I0664058

Published in West Point, New York, by Diamond Trooper Publications.

This book may be purchased in bulk for educational, business, fund-raising, or sales potional use. For information, please e-mail devinLkelly@yahoo.com.

Kelly, Devin Lawrence, 1988–
    The prison chronicles / D.K. Lawrence.

ISBN 978-0-578-01886-7

The Prison Chronicles

The Prison Chronicles

D.K. Lawrence

I met a girl who wore knee high socks and only ate the green ones. I liked the way her eyes frowned when she smiled. I think I've loved her since.

For you, Lauren.

A note to the reader:

At 19 years-old, my thoughts are raw. Do not expect the conciliatory prose of a retired professor crafting a book on philosophical musings in his quiet time. This book is written in the uncensored and unadulterated voice of a young man's mind; writing it differently would betray verisimilitude. I'd like to give readers a perspective they've never seen in literature.

The Prison Chronicles

Preface

He walks alone into solitude. Not to be followed, yet leading—leading a persuasion to serenity, to a feeling of contentment with all we are. There is no god, there is no fate, but what is, is more magnificent than anything a holy book or religion can give us. What we have is beautiful. There is a light that shines and glimmers beneath the superficial surface most people know. There is a beauty beyond Samsara, and it's hidden in the melodious mantra of nature. The atrocity of our era is the sedation of man's instinctual curiosity. I see my friends raised under the clasp of his hands, puppets on the strings of mundane. The choreographed lifestyle they will all assume, everything is so black and white. They're just going through the motions of life. And then what? Kill time. Kill time. Rather, break free. Cut loose. Realize your potential, your passion, and your niche instead of coasting through life like the self-righteous, pseudo-intellectual swine donning pretentious sweater vests, talking smart with a glass of merlot in their right hands. Anybody can pretend smart. No, go out and do! This is doing. The wandering man who ventures off into lost. Paradise lost. Oh, so serene this gentle nirvana that hums in my eyes. The hum of beauty and truth and truth is beauty and beautiful truth to that as well! Hah.

But you may never know because you fear *what*? You'll have money, you'll live fine. The only thing to fear is your hesitance to diverge from the ordinary path. So on he drifts; yet drifts deliberately, his triumph over the mold, the one who walked against the grain and found the treasure first—a realistic contentment saturated and unspoiled by the grime and muck of irrationality. He knows what he thinks and he needs nothing more. He is alone in his relinquishment of lust and greed and sinful hunger. So there he sits, paralyzed and eccentric, but he is happy because he dared to question.

1

My neck hurts. But I guess that's to be expected when you try using the door handle as a pillow. I slept in my truck last night, parked in the furthest corner of the parking lot at a rest station somewhere near Albany. I'm headed into the Adirondack region to live off the land for a week or so—grand illusions of a healthy mind body and soul meditating in solitude, eager to strip myself of the unnecessary luxuries to seek a finer appreciation for the basic needs—a humbling tie to the primitive nomadic lifestyles of our ancestors. Here it is, five a.m. and the dawn is still—a premature sun glowing over the dreary lands of upstate New York under dull skies, now a canvas for the iridescent morning rays. I reach my hand to the ignition and start my truck engine to get some heat in the cab. Still wrapped in my sleeping bag, I sit up, eyes half closed and blinking slow. The cab begins to warm up, and I unzip

my sleeping bag and swing my legs out. I turn and put my boots on loosely
just to jump out and whiz real quick, then hop back in and start to get dressed.
I'm about a three hour's drive away from the high peaks of the beautiful
Adirondacks—my escape, my next adventure.

I'm driving straight into the burning glare of the morning sun, wishing
I had brought some sunglasses, but just a bit further until I turn to head north
on I-87. On passing through upstate New York, I have this to say: he is a
lonely old man with battle scars and war stories of the industrial days when
factories prospered with men working long black hours in his mines. The
rolling lands are only weathered skin, like leather, skin once radiant and
wealthy like the cream skin of the aristocrats, but alas, his working days
caught up. And now he rocks alone to the poor poor rhythm of his wheezing
breath, rounded in the shoulder and decrepit in the joints, in his heelless
slippers and a flannel robe. Some call him miserly, but what can they expect?
This poor old man has seen it all; the innocence of hop scotch and jungle
gyms, scraped knees and puppy love; he remembers the high school frets of
debauchery and drama. He's seen the reckless days of youth abruptly faded
into new jobs with new families, and suddenly playtime was no more. Empty
obligations and boss' deadlines made him spiteful, made him neglect his
health. Now he lives in regret, thinking of the days when young ladies held his
handsome self arm in arm—kisses on his grinning cheeks. But the days of his
women in their sundresses are over, and so here sits a sad old man ticking and
tocking his heart, waiting for a death that won't come soon enough. The pitiful
man had it all, but here he withers, arthritic factories, osteoporosis in his
crumbling buildings, varicose highways and slithering roads like the wrinkles

at the nook of his eye. The poor guy smokes his cherry pipe and basks in the sweet haze of its fog, an aura that disguises an internal destruction.

In Albany I take the junction to I-87 and up to 73. It's a beautiful travel, and I'm the only one on the road, so I slow down and really watch the scenery slide past—rolling mountains and evergreen armies, rocky cliffs and run-off water paths that trickle into glass ponds. There is a long lake with a feminine slenderness that ripples with the melody of the wind, and behind it winds a train track looking very much like the Wild West of the olden days and I think to myself how I would have loved to have hopped that train route. I would have sat stoned on the edge of the flat car as the train weaved and winded its path through the mountains, all along the lake line taking me further and further into nowhere but exactly where I wanted to go. And giving this travel a Romantic raiment is the morning fog that you will only find between the delicate waking hours of the early early morn, and by late morning the cloak has disappeared and the sun shines vividly through the towering trees.

I turn down a dirt road and head into the heart of the high peaks. At the Adirondack Lodge, I park my truck, kill the engine, and lie across my seat to nap. I wake up around lunch time and decide to explore the lodge grounds a bit. I wish it were warmer, last week was great but here I am ready to head into the wild and it's back to 45 degree days and 20 degree nights. I take my book down to the small lake that sits nestled in the valley of mammoth mountains reaching far above the clouds. The lake ripples softly, protected by the mountains all around, no fears and no worries, ahh what a life! I climb atop a fallen tree and sit in its perfect seat to read and be at ease. This is going to be great…a week here in this quiet land among its tremendous beauty.

Mid afternoon, I decide to drive into Keen, the nearby town, to find somewhere to eat and stock up on supplies. I pull into a gas station and order a sub sandwich. There isn't much else I need really; my ruck sack is packed and ready for the survival journey that lies ahead. The town is a small country town, one of those back road American places where everybody knows everybody. I'm waiting in line to pay behind an old man with broad and strong shoulders draped in a worn flannel shirt. He's a farmer, hunter, and fisherman, a regular all around outdoors man, and he tells the cashier about the storm that's supposed to be rolling in. "Red skies in morning, sailors take warning. Got a big storm rollin' in, I can smell it! Supposed to rain somethin' fierce over the next couple days," he says. I had considered the possibility of rain, but my sources hadn't hinted at anything like a *storm*, as far as I knew, there were only supposed to be showers on and off throughout the week. I hop back in my truck and head back to the lodge where I eat my sub and read my books to the soft pitter patter of a young rain on my truck's roof.

The rain stops, leaving a cool humid breeze and grey clouds behind. I start to walk around the lodge area again just to see what's there. The place is deserted, except for the two cars in the main lot; it's a creepy feeling really. Near the lake are several lean-to's and behind them I come across three large canvas tents. Inside each one are three sets of bunk beds on weak and squeaky frames. The mattresses are thin, but it's got to be better than sleeping in my truck, so I decide I'll sleep in here tonight, and then I'll get a move on into the mountains in the morning.

As dusk approaches, I start to move what I'll need from my truck to the canvas tent; sleeping bag, flashlight, knife, book, and a fresh pair of socks for the morning: check. The inside of the tent is dark even in midday. I lay my sleeping bag out under the glow of the flashlight and strip down to my socks and long underwear pajamas. It's brisk in the tent, and the temperature is still dropping in the night, but my sleeping bag has pulled me through worse. Lying in my sleeping bag I begin to read in the pure silence only found in the wilderness. And then I hear something rustling my tent. My eyes pop wide and alert, my heart starts pumping fast, the shiver of adrenaline creeps its way down my spine and I sit petrified and thinking the worst; is it a bear? *An axe murderer?* I suppose our worst anticipation comes when we expect a fright, and we let our minds obsess until the mental fear has far surpassed the physical fright or pain of the actual startling. Oh, such an obsession rushes into my whirling mind with each passing second—the whips and winds of electric thought! The stillness was prolonged until a second rustling, this time behind me and now more noticeable. I dare say my heart's loud pounding would rat me out and I would be devoured, if not by this beast, then by my own slipping mind. I flash the light on the canvas flaps at the entrance of the tent. In the light I see it is only the wind blowing in the flaps, rustling them against one another. Cheer for the slipping mind of silly me, petrified in false fear, yet I am still not comforted. Each rustle thereafter I tell myself, it is only the wind! But still I lie tense with ready eyes, my knife open just in case. I decide to put my headphones in and drift off to my music to keep from obsessing over the haunting rustlings, but it only makes the paranoia worse. To not hear a potential predator or threat approaching violates all logic and law relating to

13

survival, and only one song in I turn the iPod off. Eventually I manage to coax my mind to rest and finally sleep.

2

One thing I love about nature is waking up with the dawning sun and singing birds. I wake up early, before seven, and pack my things up to take back to the truck. I eat a small breakfast (a banana and some nuts) as I pack the ruck sack up ready and eager to start living off the land. I shoulder the ruck sack, sling my rifle over my neck, and venture off into solitude.

Over the trails hangs a thin morning haze, wet and cool and just incredible. I walk the trails through the valleys, really absorbing the amazing land. The sights are tremendous, winding trails through friendly trees that tip their hats and greet you hello as you walk by. The upturned stumps are blanketed in a vibrant green moss. Look out into the forest and you'll see the reddened tree trunks hugged together like affectionate families that play and laugh and love their children. It's an ideal world for them in here, at least on the surface. I come across a running stream, wide and healthy and crashing over a rocky fall. The soothing static of the crashing water and rustling tree branches is something everybody needs to enjoy. The falling water gives me the peace of mind to just let my thoughts free, open the Pandora's Box and clear my mind of all that it is—let me enjoy the wonderful nothingness while it's here. I take a seat on a rounded rock that seems to smile at me with chubby cheeks—a Buddha belly boulder. I take a bud of green out of my pocket and smoke it to grey, and now I'm feeling green and great and something poetic. In the stream are sickly, almost deflated looking rocks for me to jump across, and on these starving rocks, little roots are trying to grow. On the other side of the stream, I put my headphones in and let my steps fall rhythmically to the song. And pretty soon the marijuana has me dancing along the trail and singing songs at the top of my lungs because there is nobody around and it feels so *good* to laugh without the looks. And with each song comes a new dance or a new thought or a new mood, from stoned to high to contented—this is so *nice*.

Now through the tree tops I can see the bulging shoulders of the slumbering giants, their peaks stick up through the high haze with a wise divinity. And now I'm starting to ascend the gentle slope of the mountains where already the air is becoming cooler. Here I see the first tickling snowfall since March or so. Thick gentle snowflakes fall on the whims of the wind and land on evergreen needles like a winter wonderland, but it's almost May, now I'm glad I wore long underwear! Here I see my first fork in the trail, signs pointing to this sight or that, and to the left lies an open clearing and a tranquil lake where the sun beams down its pretty light and gives the land a vibrant sparkle that the marijuana makes a poem or a painting or some sort of art out of. The lake is lush and deep dark blue with tiny waves that roll curiously at my feet. Around the lake is the luscious greenery of post cards and picture paintings, and I think to myself that this is what I came for! I walk the sand around the perimeter of the lake to the opposite end where I see an opening in the woods. An hour or so of clearing it up and it will be a perfect campsite for the night.

I make a game out of my chores under the blissful tilt of the marijuana, clearing the site, collecting firewood, and filling up on water. In the woods I look for dead tree limbs to break and cut and I make a small pile of firewood (too small). With the breeze blowing off the lake, I can't get the fire started and I'm starting to frustrate. I have my lighter burning through the tinges of tinder and lining the kindling logs in embers, but the flames just will not catch. I move my tinder and kindling pile into a ditch 'neath the upturned roots of a fallen tree where the wind won't interrupt, and after twenty minutes more of fretting, I get the twigs to catch. I let it build up just a bit, and carefully move the burning kindling to my original tinder set in logs. The logs catch and I have a weak fire, but it's fire nonetheless. I grab a trunk I had fallen earlier and begin to split it into logs, but it seems like every time I split a new log, the fire is hungry for it and I just can't get a pile built up. I call this my first mistake in the wild, and make mental note for tomorrow. But by now it's dusk and night sneaks up quick here in the mountains, so I lay out my tent and start to set it up. I watch the sun peeking at me from behind the crest of two mountains toward the west and I laugh a quiet laugh, thinking "peek-a-boo, sun. I see you!" but I know he won't be there for long and when he's

17

gone it'll be back to the wont of the scary night, and me here alone means my imagination is not my friend.

I'm too quickly running through my pathetic wood pile and regretting not having started sooner. But the tent will keep me dry and my bag will keep me warm and that's the most important thing right now. The fire simmers to a hot glow come ten o'clock, but I'm dog tired and ready for sleep—no rustling canvas tonight, only the rustling leaves overhead and the wind beating the sides of my tent. I fall asleep at peace and really happy, feeling a sense of purity in my seclusion.

3

It's 2:11 a.m. and I've just cracked awake to the thunderous sound of a breaking bough. It sounded like a whole trunk was ferociously snapped at the spine with the gracelessness of a maniacal giant out hungry and on the prowl, searching for little boys to feed on like the haunting story tales we told as children. And here I am curled up in a ball, sleeping bag pulled up past my chin like I'm living in a nightmare and I just want to scream *"Mom?!"* It could have been a twig snapping for all I know, but my heightened senses are telling me to wake up and be alert and just try and *survive* at all costs. Oh, I'm such an animal! An insect, even, will squirm and fight until it's dying time when trapped in a puddle of water, and why? Does such a thing think "I have a wife and kids back home!" or "I'm too young to die right now, I haven't seen the world, I haven't seen Rome or the pyramids or even the *Pacific!*" But something has them clawing and fighting right up until their dying demise, a neurological spark of survival above all, survive to reproduce! say Darwin. Well, here I am, an ant under the shadow of the monster's stomping foot, fear and adrenaline—neurological spark—coursing through my veins, preparing for the fight or flight battle that will surely ensue when this monster reveals itself. I lie, balled up, listening acutely for the next snapping bough, wishing I weren't here. *What am I doing? What is the point? Tomorrow I will surely head for the safe comforts of home!* I want to be 12 years ago, I want to sit at my kitchen table sipping hot cocoa after sledding, wearing long pajama pants and socks on little feet that swing free in the air, not yet reaching the floor. I want to be back in my kitchen with my mom making mac 'n cheese, me and my bro bickering like brothers do over who went faster (I did!). I want my mom telling us to stop it and to be nice to one another because some day we're gonna miss each other. And here is that day; here I am wishing I were back home with Mom and little brother. I want to be 12 years ago, sitting at that kitchen table swinging my little legs freely telling Mom how fast I went zooming down that hill, "and then I hit the jump going backwards! I went way higher than Cam!" as Mom puts the bowl of mac 'n cheese down, cut up hot dogs all mixed in the way we like 'em—Thanks Mom! I want to be warm and safe and protected from harm by the hug of my great mother and I think, if only she were here to slay this lumbering giant, this awful beast! She would too, that's how great she is. But I'm alone and waiting tense to hear the roar of some black bear that smells my peanut butter and hears the pounding of my chest. It never comes, just a sick tree, a dying man in the old forest, falling broken to his grave with a final *bang!*

The morning sun makes wonderful out of terrible, my violent nightmare now a pretty dream. There is the lake again, and the luminous mountains, tops hidden by the clouds. Today will be a day of hunting, trapping, and firewood fetching—hopefully some cooking too. The early morning is alive with critters, and I decide it's best to get an early start hunting rather than worry about the traps just yet. I shoulder my loaded .22 magnum rifle and head out away from civilization. I walk an hour north, stoned and loving nature, until I find a ridge where I can sit and watch over the land below. I see the chipmunks playing; I hear the song birds chirping, but I'm looking for at least a squirrel. I hear their calls, but I don't see any yet. I sit leaning against a stump and reading my book, glancing up after every page for some sort of commotion that means dinner. An hour passes and nothing is close enough or big enough. I've been keeping my eye on a squirrel for a while now, and he's bouncing closer and closer in range. Finally I think I have him. He's fifty yards out and sitting with his breakfast in the crook of a tree. I'm not loving this, but he's my dinner and this is how the world works. Forget about the idealistic anti-war anti-establishment bullshit. Yes, in a utopian world we would all hug and sing around the campfire and be happy and nice with 0 violence and 100 love. But we're only human and humans are only animals and animals kill and prey and feed, driven by an innate greed. Well, now I'm hungry and I'm greedy because of it and I'm using whatever I can to earn my food. I put the crosshairs on the neck of the squirrel and watch his little whiskers and those cute, dumb eyes. I take a deep breath, hold it for a second, and let it out slow and once it's gone I squeeze the trigger. The gun rings out into the open forest and the squirrel drops twenty feet to the dead leaves that litter the ground with a dull thud, agonizingly withering its tiny muscles—my meal. In all the squirrels I've killed (always eaten) one thing has never gotten easier. It pains me to watch and sends my heart somersaulting to see the squirrels flexing and crawling helplessly in their last breaths of life, their chattering scream piercing me, as though begging me to help its poor soul, to say one last prayer for him and his family—as though he doesn't know that I am his killer.

Strange to think about eating the muscles that moved the squirrel you watched at play. But in the end, I am hungry and I'm only human. And humans are only animals and animals have to eat somehow—because if I don't then I am the victim. Call it greedy, but greed is our primitive nature. Say that we, as humans, are better than that and I will say we aren't. Nor should we pretend we are. We are only as good as our behaviors, not our idealistic thoughts. Note also: I am talking about hunting for food necessary to my survival. I am not justifying fits of rage based on our primitive greed-based emotions (jealousy, anger, narcissism) that harm other people.

I walk up to the base of the tree where the squirrel lies (now dead) bleeding at the base of his skull. The hollow point bullet mushroomed out to tear the entire right side of his face open. The squirrel couldn't have suffered much; the short-lived withering was probably only electrical short signals from a severed lower spine. A squirrel doesn't make much of a meal, so I head back up to the ridge, hoping for more. But the hours pass and the pages turn and still nothing. By noon time I get up and head back to the campsite to try my luck in traps.

Back at the camp I realize that skinning and dressing the squirrel and collecting firewood are going to take much longer than expected, and suddenly my setting traps isn't top priority. Grey skies and jagged clouds glare mean at me and make the sun shine sharp through crooked sneers. The rain is on its way, and by the looks of these thuggish clouds, it's gonna be a hell of a storm. The wind picks up with that fresh pre-rain smell to it, and I start cutting at the skin of the squirrel. Squirrel skin is surprisingly tough, and my knife struggles to make the first incision. Once I have that started, the process of skinning it should only take a half an hour. I cut down along the sternum and through its pelvis and peel back the skin to cut at the membrane. Once I have skinned out the legs, I pull and the skin peels away from the muscular skeleton, all the way down the tail and all the way through the face, whiskers and eye holes and all. For my purposes, there's no need to gut the insides. I fillet strips of meat off the back and thighs and any scraps I can get at here and there, then chuck the corpse far out into the lake—the last thing I need are coyotes or foxes or bears around my campsite. I wash the small strips of meat, maybe three ounces, in the lake water to remove the blood and hair mess, and then wrap the strips in a plastic bag. It's only mid afternoon, but the clouds are dense and dark and ominous. I start to quicken my pace collecting firewood, jogging from tree to tree, I cut down six thick branches and thin trunks, all mostly dead, and drag them back together to the campsite. I quickly cut the thinnest branch into logs and set them leaning against one another, ready to light. I gather dried leaves and browned bark shavings for tinder and, deciding not to waste any time, take it right to the ditch to block the wind. The tinder catches, but my kindling sticks won't and now I'm getting nervous. I hear the

23

thunder rolling far away, but thunder travels fast and unpredictably and who knows what is going to happen. Again I feel that regretful fear begin to knock at my door, but no time to answer; there are more important things at stake.

I get a stick burning and throw more leaves into the pile to fuel it, then cautiously bring it over to the waiting logs. The fire is burning weakly, and I'm thinking the wind is going to blow it right out under the logs. I shield it with my body until I notice the logs themselves starting to ember and smoke, then it's back to cutting the rest of the branches and trunks. The fire is cooking steadily now, but the wind is blowing the smoke almost horizontally and I know the storm ain't too far off. My tent is ready, ruck sack organized, so I decide that I had better eat while there is time. I remove the squirrel strips and lay them in the tin can, then hang it on a branch over the fire. I burn the strips until I think they're safe to eat, and then I enjoy the succulent meal, the first thing I have had to eat in almost two days. With the squirrel meat, I have peanut butter, high in calories and fat and a much needed boost in energy and morale. Hardly full, but feeling better, I continue cutting logs to build a pile. Halfway through my third branch, the rain drops start to come. Thick ugly rain drops at first, falling slowly here and there, but only one minute later and my hair is dripping and the trees are pattering. I throw my tarp around my logs to keep them as dry as possible and crawl into my tent, shielded by the rain but still wet. With the heavy raindrops thumping at my tent, I feel a sort of coziness I hadn't expected. I've always loved thunderstorms, their power and their brilliant bleakness. And here I am, cold legs in my warm sleeping bag, the soothing crackle of the rain on my tent, and a new meal in my belly, I curl up and smile all to myself. There will be no predators out for me tonight. All there is, is this peaceful storm and me alone and nature all around. I curl up in my bag, grinning at the brink of comfort. And then the roaring clash of thunder over head nearly deafens me and I remember that this is a storm, that this is the wild, and that there is no such thing as safety or "cozy." The lightning poses a new threat. But at the moment, there is nothing I can do about it, except sleep and let whatever will happen, happen.

4

The thunder was clashing all night—booming thunder that shook the trees at their trunks. But I'm awake now, and I open my tent flap to see the damage done. The ground is sodden and everything is soaked, including my logs, even with the tarp around them. But the only thing I can do is go about my day, which means hunting, trapping, and firewood collecting. So I shoulder my rifle and head back out toward the same ridge. The ground is laden in a frost décor, and all the plants and leaves are too. It's a pretty picture, and I can't pass through it angry like I am. I stop to appreciate all that is around me. I may be hungry, I may be tired and sore as well, but I knew this trip would be no vacation. The purpose of this trip was to see and appreciate and *live* in these pretty pictures, away from it all, stripped of the luxury commodities that pervert consumerism into an epidemic. And now I see the simple beauty at the root of anything, me stripped to my basic needs, I see delectable in squirrel meat (what I wouldn't do for a peanut butter sandwich right now!), I taste water as it was meant to be tasted (nectar of the gods!). And a safe place to stay? I've experienced the likes of not having one, and I'm all the more appreciative for home. So here I'm walking into a hunt, and I'm so centered on only me, my aching neck, my cold body, my blistered feet and empty belly, that I can't see the beauty all around me—like reading poetry to the kids who just don't *care*. It's a travesty, and I can't let me go on this way. I take a seat and close my eyes in meditation. Ease my breathing, lost in a realm where body is suspended in the welk of mind, a spiritual universe black and dense and warm and soothing. So I leave my physical hurt in this nothing (anything) bath to heal while I open my eyes and let my mind relish the elements. And to help, I pull my pipe out and begin to smoke, eased by the green of the nature and my herb, now I am where I should be; now I am living this poem!

As I'm sitting on that Buddha belly rock, I see a rabbit in the shade of an evergreen branch, hopping here and there to nibble on some green of its own. I think about death and killing and violence and I don't want to have to kill the thing, but it will be done. I thumb the safety off and raise my rifle slowly, line the cross hairs up on one of the poor bunny's ears and take a deep breath in: hold it for a second, then let it out and let my sights fall slowly with my sinking chest, and just as the cross hairs touch the base of poor bunny's skull, I pull the trigger. The shot rings hollow through the mountains and poor bunny leaps three feet in the air and takes off, but doesn't make it twenty feet before it falls on its side, one last helpless kick of its legs. I jog over to it, dead with open eyes, lying on its side in a grassy patch. The grass is soft and frosted over except in the small ring around the dead body of the still warm rabbit. It is an amazing scene, miraculous really, and now I'm wishing I had brought a camera because words will do this picture no justice. The rabbit will be a heartier meal than the skinny squirrel last night, and so I grab the thing by the strong legs and head back to camp. I'm lucky to have gotten the kill so early today, and now I have time to dabble in the trapping game.

With some wire, I rig up three squirrel poles: a long stick with alternating wire nooses along the way (lean them against a tree and the squirrels will climb up, getting their neck caught in the noose. After some struggling, the squirrel will lose its grip and fall to be hanged by the wire. Squirrels aren't smart, and I've seen people catch three or four at a time with this method (I guess they aren't quick learners)). With the squirrel poles positioned, I make my way over to the marshy land near the pond to set some snares in the runways through the grass. I've never had luck with trapping, and I'm hoping that somehow I'll be more successful this time.

By now it's afternoon and the sun is actually warm, the storm must have prefaced a warm front, and the golden shine of the sun and its warming rays are a much needed morale booster. Back at the camp, I strip down to my shorts and begin to dress and fillet the rabbit. The sun is blazing on my back, and the warmth is so comforting and uplifting. The rabbit skin pulls off easily and I'm able to strip more meat off of its strong legs than I could on the squirrel. I put the meat in the bag and start to cut more wood for a fire. My already cut logs have dried considerably in the open sun, and in the woods, the high branches already crack and break dry, good for burning. Maybe it's my uplifted spirit (marijuana and happy sun) but the work seems to fly right by.

Nothing is so dreary and melancholy as the first frigid day, and today I spark up the kindling with ease. I have a small fire burning steadily to help warm the place up even more and dry my wet ruck. I take the meat and tin down to the lake.

The lake is clear and crisp and inviting, and well…I'm here, I might as well make the most of it. I strip my shorts and wade into the cold water, but the cold isn't unpleasant. In fact, it tingles and tickles every point on my naked skin. I duck my head underwater and let the lake wash and slide over me. The sun is sparkling right off the surface, giving the lake a magical shimmer and I'm convinced this lake is *healing* me. Each droplet serenades me softly and sings me aware—aware of the nature of being, aware of my own selfishness, and aware of resolution. I'm drowning in rebirth, nourished by this fresh water sanctum. Air is whole with the subtle perfume of purity and resilience; it bathes me in freedom, relinquishing sinful desire. Each breath is visceral and meditational and synchronized with the hum of *it.* What is *it? It* is the realm of The Illustrious Buddha's nirvana; *it* is the relinquishment of suffering and the exploration of subconscious potential, *it* is "Om" and the vibration of verisimilitude, *it* is the revelation of unity between mind-body-soul and the universe encompassing. And once I have experienced *it,* I hesitate to return to the plight of society. The beauty of self-awareness! Its serenity and stillness and I just want to lean back and be a part of the greater whole, and I want the greater whole to be a part of me, of this, of *it!* I want the world I was born into, not the world perverted by structure, disillusionment, and spite. I will roam unconfined by servitude against all things which disagree with justice and ethics. *"Non serviam!"* This is where I belong: one with time and nature and the world. And should that be more than enough? Who I am contradicts what I am told to be—Thoreau would be proud! And sinking back into layers of consciousness: the universe is so simple at first; it is effervescent in my soul. I am alive! I have found *it*! It: the answer to the desolate void. It: reality. It: awareness. It: actualization.

I walk back to the shore, nude and dripping, and finish washing the meat and tin while drying in the warming sun. The air is cool and snaps and stings at my wet chest but I'm alive and new and free! I wander around the camp site in the nude for a while, smoking, singing, and dancing to my iPod around the fire like I'm some kind of native nomad calling for rain or begging for a good hunt. But that's not what I'm doing. I'm dancing and really just enjoying myself.

But the elevated feeling is fleeting, soon dissipated with the prospect of survival. The ability to sustain such elation is a mark of men far greater and wiser than myself. For me, it's back to the grind of living. Enlightenment is elusive at nineteen years old.

The fire is burning steadily, but my pile is dwindling, so I get to work cutting more logs. Still naked, I'm hacking and breaking at the branches, sweating at the brow and hunched over in the shoulders. My chest is red and heaving now, and pumped strong with the blood flow from the exercise. I stand up, knife in one hand, log in the other, strong shoulders hanging off the sides of my back and breathing chest, sweat dripping down my nose and to the ground—and I think to myself what this must look like to an artist. The naked male body is a handsome thing in all its rips and rounds of muscle. Here I'm standing, lean and long, my wrestler's shape, under the hot sun making my

30

neck turn red like my chest, I'm thinking about the ancient Greek or Roman art, the athlete's graceful fortitude, a conditioned body and a strong mind to drive it. There really is a deep beauty in a healthy body, beyond aesthetics even. A strong body is evidence of hard work or time spent sacrificing and learning and overcoming physical adversity, all essential foundations of discipline and gratitude. Many people have it in mind or body, one or the other, but to find harmony between the two is something impressive. A part of me wants to say eat, drink, be merry. Get fat and be happy to eat, but realize, that without prior sacrifice, the joys of eating will go undiscovered. The same principle stands for over-indulging in anything. For example, to a glutton, eating is mundane, and potentially worse than the misery of starvation (self-consciousness, embarrassment, depression, not to mention all the health issues prevalent in the overly fat or obese). Yes, a conditioned body is just as essential as a sharp mind.

I throw the log I'm holding onto the fire and put my head phones in to dance and sing some more. Out here I can yell and scream and be as crazy as I want and the only ones to listen are the mountains and the chickadees, and they only laugh along as my background choir (chickadees). Here I am, naked in the forest under the cradling sun and blanket of the fire, singing and calling out into the lively woods, playing with my sounds like a curious baby does before he learns to form his words—talk about mother nature! What a sight this must be! To watch me from the outside, I would think I were some kind of demented.

It's bear country and bear season, and why not make friends with these cuddly critters? (Oh yeah, 'cause the last guy who tried that got eaten…painfully. New game plan.) So I call out (as they say one should make noise constantly to keep the bear from sneaking up and being startled into a fit of rage resulting in my dismemberment). I'm saying, "Heyyyy bearrrr! Come out and plaaaaayyy bearrrr!" Well, now I'm cold and my clothes have been warming and drying by the fire, and when I slide my long underwear on, it's another surge of "oh, THIS IS WHY I'M HERE!" I nearly melt right there. And here it's nearly snuck up on me: this moment of ecstasy where life makes sense and I finally feel like I know myself and I say to myself, "people are weird, but I like them for the most part." This is doing, this is getting up and going out and putting my thoughts/ideas into action. Too many people sit around in their pretentious sweater vests reading books they pretend to understand, books they pretend they can relate to, and everybody has something "profound" to say on it. But it's all just a bunch of pricks with their panties in a bunch using big words 'cause they want everyone to think they're as smart as they think they are. Well, anyone can sit around and pretend smart. But go out and do! Go out and live your life and put your thoughts to the test! Go out and live a *story!* We all sit around watching cool movies and reality shows…why aren't we, ourselves, living these lives? We have 100 years until we die! Are you going to sit back and let the tide carry you in and out through life? Or are you going to get out and live your passion? Challenge yourself and find out what you're made of, live a story you can tell your grandkids!

Now I'm grilling up the rabbit and wishing I had some Italian marinade, or teriyaki. I take out my peanut butter (almost gone) and when the rabbit is cooked through I smear peanut butter on the strips and eat them like that. It's no Taco Bell, but out here it's delicious. And by the time I've finished my savory meal, it's dusk and I can already see stars in the clear darkening sky. It's still warm out near the fire, and once I've piled up enough wood, I just lie down inside the tent to read and write and just be here, immersed in this desolate haven.

tired trees
  weep crystal tears
that freeze on their
  cold, weathered skin.
the gray skies and barren branches
make cold
      the sentiments of these elderly beasts.
  and if you ask them for directions…
        they just glare with snarled, knotted expressions.
  then they whisper rumors about you in the night.
scary, twisted, frames that claw at the moon.
                        and they come alive at midnight.
old souls that groan mean—scarred and sore with crippled bones.
  arthritis. osteoporosis.
    "drink your milk!" i scream.
so they whisper louder to drown my hope.
    loud, harsh snaps and whistles. scary ghosts
    that go >crack< in the night and hiss obscenities.
brisk breath that snaps and stings and smells like scotch—
                            and gets me drunk
                      so that my world is rewinding
                  into a frightening nostalgia
              where monsters lurk
          and howl hungry for
      little children.

this is the first time i realize i am alone—this is solitude.

and now my
            mindisrunning
                  running around in terror and ecstasy.

33

it is a callow ping of fear in the mind.
    the fantastic ideas that convince my id that
        there are ferocious creatures about.
           and i'm nowhere near home or safety or help and
             i am on my own
             so my paranoia rushes
             and my body paralyzes
               and my breathing sprints
           creating little puffs of ghosts that float and engulf my body
                ::the void::
             that melancholy cloud that
               exposes ubiquitous beauty in every scene.
             this must be nirvana.

and this is when i crawl out of my tent to observe the beauty.
                                     to live this poem.
    no writing yet, only doing.
        experiencing.
           the landscape is too beautiful.
           rich dark blue sea over head,
               its smooth rippling in the moonlight.
    rolling hills of giants in slumber.
               grandfather trees that hug me goodnight.
               the quiet loud serenity of the wind's whining whistles.
                           and me content.

And when it's night time through and through, I'm lying in the heat of the fire under wise stars and wondering about what this world is or isn't, the kind of light metaphysical "what-if" stuff that sends me 'round in circles, no start, no end, and certainly no conclusion. And it's just so peaceful out here, just me and the crackling fire, like an old friend with his tangible warmth and whispering gibberish, so I think I'll just sleep here under the stars tonight, like a cowboy on our next frontier. I throw two logs on and pull my sleeping bag out of the tent. I close my eyes and sleep a beautiful sleep with beautiful dreams, just happy to be doing what I want to be doing.

5

The next morning even before dawn, the birds are already out and about. I wake up to the lovely sound of a crow cawing incessantly. I'm still tired, and I want to sleep, but the forest is alive and already hustling and bustling. Somewhere in the distance I hear a woodpecker's staccato machine gun sound, and it really reminds me of where I am, away from society and encapsulated in this nature wonderland. The fire has died down, and the wood is merely glowing, I'll have to start another one this afternoon. Sleeping outside of the tent has made me wake up even before I usually do, daylight hasn't even cracked yet, it's that sad time of the morning, the transition from dark to dawn. Like when you stay up all night with friends and you never want that night to end, but somehow the sun always seems to come up telling you it has to end sometime. It's the so-depressing hour of four a.m. and the shadows are long and sharp, cold and ominous. To think of the highs from yesterday and contrast them with the dooming haze of this dark morning leaves me with an omnipresent emptiness in the pit of my gut. Forget drugs: in life alone, for every high you'll hit that low. But the sun comes up quick and soon it's yellow morning. I stroll down to the lake and fill up my tin, then head back to camp to grab my rifle and weed, then it's off to the ridge.

Today proves to be my best hunt. Maybe it was because I was up an hour earlier, but at the ridge I shot three squirrels, all one shot one kill, and hustled back to my camp with a newfound hop in my step—tonight is gonna be a feast! So immediately I start skinning and dressing the squirrels and wondering how many more I might have caught in my traps. As that early morning fog begins to dissipate the place gets warmer and I shed my Carhart. I finish the filleting and put all of the scraps together in the plastic bag and seeing all of that meat together only keeps me smiling and eager for the feast tonight. I decide to let the traps sit a while longer while I get started on the firewood. Out here, one really needs to keep up on all these things. I came in thinking I'd have all sorts of time to myself to read and write and think, but I suppose in a way, just living off the land in itself is meditating for me.

I spend all morning on the firewood job until life in the wilderness turns from glorified and serene, to brutal and miserable. My hands are blistered, my feet are wet and cold, I have no fire yet, and I slammed my thumb with a rock. I'm shivering, hungry, and starting to get dehydrated and I decide that today has got to be my last day. I'll end the survival game with an afternoon feast and begin to walk back to the truck in the morning. But by the third time I hit that same thumb and I can't even hold the knife tight in my ripped and bleeding hands, I decide that I ain't gonna make it through the night. I just want to be *home* because eventually solitude catches up to you. And when your hands are bloody broken and bruised, the survival game turns into the survival reality. Besides, I've gotten what I came looking for, and that is peace of mind—seclusion for a bit—away from the world and all alone. Part of the motivation behind this adventure was to make me more grateful for all I had back home, and by now I've reached that point. I want to be back at RIT causin' ruckus with my coy antics. I want to be in my warm bed with Keven to tuck me in telling me, "Sweet dreams, Lopez!" I want to see my lil bro walk in the front door and say to me, "Buddy, I'll kick your ass!" with that cocky smirk he wears so well. I want a shower and I want to be warm with no more misery, because I had so much back home and now I realize it. I've gotten what I came looking for, and now I just want to go *home!*

And by noon I'm checking all the traps with disappointment. I've never had luck in trapping, and today is no different. So I check each empty trap with a sad sigh and then I take them down and ball the wires up. Oh well, I have a feast of squirrels from this morning, can't complain about that.

So back at camp I've got a fire going and I'm roastin' up my squirrel lunch. I've already rolled the tent up, the sleeping back is packed, and all I'm gonna do is eat my meal, absorb the last of nature's beauty, then be on my way back to my good old truck, back on the road for one last day, then back *home!*

I shoulder my ruck sack and eat the cooked squirrel strips out of the bag along the way. It's two o'clock, and I won't make it back before night unless I put some skip in my step, and I don't want to be stuck walking the eerie trails past dusk. And five miles into my hike back, I'm at a fork in the road with a sign that reminds me that I still haven't climbed a mountain. The sign says "Mt. Marcy----6.2 miles" with an arrow pointing down another path. Mt. Marcy is New York's highest peak, and what kind of man would I be if I came and conquered all I have so far, and failed to sit atop the highest mountain in New York? Well I don't know, because there's no way I'm not getting to the top! So here I go and set the bar higher, knowing that every high has its low and though it's gonna suck tonight, tomorrow will be all the more worth it when I'm sitting on the highest peak of New York. So I hang a sharp left and head back into the wilderness for one last night.

I'm close to the base of the mountain now, and I decide to walk up until dusk before I set up a camp. I've finished my squirrel, but I have my one bag of trail mix and that's gonna be my meal for the climb tomorrow. So I hump up the trail, ruck sack choking at my shoulders, until dusk time where I set up the tent and lay out my sleeping bag. I don't even bother with a fire; though, it would really help to boost morale. My hands can't take more wood splitting.

6

The next morning I wake up with the birds bright and early. I consider leaving my rucksack behind, only climbing with my Camelback and Carhart; knife, trail mix, marijuana, iPod, and tape recorder in the pockets. But if I were to get lost, I could be screwed without my ruck, maybe I should take it. Then again, where's the triumph if no risks are taken?! Fuck it, I'm taking my chances! So I pack up my ruck sack and lean it in a ditch, and I'm off to high peaks and high times.

The trails are just marvelous in the morning fog, green leaves and red trunks, rolling hills and surling streams; and again I'm thinking *why don't I have a camera?!* I'm treading on the dirt paths that thud with my steps, the paths that weave and wind through this mystical underbrush, and the only sounds are the washing waters and the happy birds and my own steps and breaths. This is nature, this is why I went left instead of right last night, this is why I took the Mt. Marcy route. The trail starts to steepen, and with higher heights comes even more amazing scenery, and at the top of one such hill I sit to rest and tighten my boots and light my pipe to turn this world into something *poetic* I tell myself (though it's there already). The marijuana is not so much a sorry escape as it is a heightened state of altered chemistry. Because that's all our existence is, our thoughts, emotions, and ultimately our actions boil down to brain chemistry. And now I want my brain chemistry telling me the world is great! I want to *feel* the music in my curious knees. I want my mind rolling with Keatsian lines, an expanded consciousness and heightened awareness to all that lies beneath the boring surface. I want to watch this beauty become a juxtaposed reality where the trees wave hi and the critters laugh alongside me. And I even consider eating my mushrooms, but I can't afford to have a bad trip out lost in the wilderness, and that would just be stupid. So it's easy Mary Jane for me. I take a breath and hold my lungs full and as this haze wholly disperses my gaze falls fully immersed in this painted scene for me to play. I'm on my way up the trail singing loud. Soon I come to a bridge across roaring white water and I just pause to watch the river with stoned focus to the melody of its own slow tune like metabolism rhythm.

Further up the mountain, there is a gentle and mystifying snow fall, silent and serene and I'm wondering, *am I really here?* The temperature has dropped and I can see my breath. Snow crunches under my drifting footsteps as I trudge through this softened quietude. Deciduous trees are scarce up here, now it's mostly evergreens, like Christmas in the forest. So I'm thinking that maybe all I need to do in this white trimmed world is stop my reading and just *look* at the words because where ever I look, there's something to be seen.

41

Immersed in this movie or picture, whatever it is. I can't say *life* because that's too specific, or maybe too vague—can it be both at the same time?

Or something. My mind has left my hurting body. My mind is rolling, stream of consciousness, stream of water that rushes over and under darkened crevices, exploring new ideas. And now the trail is just incredible, the upturned trunks with their long winding roots, like snakes beneath my feet. But these aren't evil snakes, nay! I need not fear these snakes, for they are the friendly type that slide alongside and slur their esses when they say "hello ssssir!" The chirping birds that sing just for me to dance—this is like a Disney movie, and everybody is happy and everybody knows the words and we all sing together. There is no questioning life for them. Why should there be? They're *happy!*

And look at how those rocks line up all in order and just for me to hop the roaring streams that dare cross my path! So I hop from head to happy head and when I make that final jump onto the other side I see my happy world has left me—a border separating good and evil, "oh how trite!" I yell. "You measly forest and your clichéd plots! I saw it coming." They were expecting to scare me, but I am high and see right through it…nice try! That intuitive underlying sight that exposes everyone and everything for what they are as only marijuana can! Well, I sir, will not fall victim! Keep your chin up, kid, and carry on. Do you see how powerful the mind is? A disciplined mind will give you the confidence to always push through, persevere. And for twenty minutes my legs are aching, my feet are blistered, and my muscles are starved of energy and nutrients, but only for twenty minutes. And after that I let my mind wander while my body clicks on, a mindless machine that knows only the droning wisdom of step-step-step-step.

The next stream has no path across, no bridge or staggering rocks, and as I approach it, I'm babbling something into my tape recorder about ice cream cones and nipples (the mountain tops). There's no way to cross except to walk right through the rushing water, bending low so I don't get swept away by the undertow (Under Toad). And as I'm crossing the knee deep water, I start to slip and catch my balance, but my glove slips out of my pocket and starts to float away and here I was muttering something about how talking is just as good as writing into my tape recorder, but now all the tape recorder hears is, "FUCK, FUCK my GLOVE! Ah, shit!" and I walk down river to where my glove is caught on a branch, muttering something about how funny this is going to be to listen to on the tape recorder, me being all poetic "the whispery trees like giggling children in a church communion...FUCK, my GLOVE!"

And as I reach down to pick my glove out of the water, wouldn't you know it; my tape recorder slips out of my hoodie pocket and drowns to the bottom. So there go all my recordings, my thoughts and sounds.

But I finish crossing, noticing suddenly how painful the cold water has become on my feet, like stinging needles at every prick of skin. And my wet feet are going to mean bigger blisters too. But I feel so *adventurous* crossing the river alone in the wilderness, like I'm in some action movie. It's when I was ten and wanted to play Army or pretend I was hunting through the jungles, and now it's real and just as cool, like big kid playtime with the mountains as my jungle gym! So on the other side, I smoke and carry on.

Now I'm pretty high (pun) and there is snow all around. The trail is all an ice bridge, slippery and packed snow that leads the winding way up to the summit. I can see the summit now, off the cliff to my right (as the trail curves around) and just from here it's so amazing and I can't wait 'til I'm on top! But by now my hunger is catching up to me, I'm out of water in my Camelback, and my aching muscles are beginning to feel the heaviness of not eating. Anybody who has experienced it before knows the feeling, the sucked out feeling where your muscles ache just to sit *still—j*ust to be *still* is a strain. And here I am trying to reach the summit of Mt. Marcy, a mile up in the air too, where oxygen begins to thin. So now my legs have that burning soreness—my never quitting legs that motored me through the yellow heart and the iron veins of America—that, too, ate the night, the long desolate America through Sanford and Shamford and Blamford and Shitsburg. And now they've got that uncontrollable shake and cramp like I've just finished sets of squats, but I haven't, it's the dehydration, my starving muscles, and now it's the thinning air. It's during these nagging times when you begin to question why you're putting yourself through such hardships, and it's during these times that you have to be able to reassure yourself of why you're doing it. There is no time for wavering, defeat is like water at a door, open the door just a little, and the water will force it all the way open to flood your mind and drown your dreams. And just when you think you've reached your breaking point, know this: you haven't!

So I push on, remembering that it will only suck for twenty minutes before my mind wanders off and leaves my body to be a machine, that step-step-step-step chord. At the last stretch before the summit, I'm above the tree

44

line and I can see for mile after beautiful mile through the entire high peaks region. From here, the world is a microcosm, chocolate chip volcanoes in a cookie-dough desert, like cheese craters of the moon. I'm eating some of my trail mix for a final boost in energy, sitting on a barren patch of rock and overlooking the world, and suddenly I see another climber coming up the trail behind me. I watch him for a bit, and when he finally reaches me I greet him with a "good morning, sir!"

"Oh, hey there. Nice day for a climb, eh? I wish it weren't so overcast tho."

I hadn't expected anyone to be climbing today, especially not this time of the year, but here he is, and he seems friendly enough. We talk like strangers about the weather at first. But soon we're talking like good friends. It's funny how close people feel after they have endured a hardship together. I've always said that's why two strangers at wrestling camp can bond so quickly, there is so much respect between them both for the inevitable suffering and undying perseverance the sport demands. And even further, two soldiers back from a war, or even just boot camp, also feel an uncanny bond between them. So I'm here talking chummy with the man as we approach the summit. He's from Canada, eh: talks like, "owt and abowt." He's in his fifties, and he's got that same *live life to the fullest* spark about him that I seem to find in all my strangers on these types of adventures. He tells me about climbing Kilimanjaro, how he climbed it just last year with his daughter. I get the impression that he's a caring family man, but I find out that he's not married anymore, and he's probably never felt whole since, poor guy. And maybe his mountain climbing and bungee jumping are just temporary escapes from his

45

lonely life, a quick lived high before it's back to the monotony of everyday life (I speak from experience). So now we're climbing the icy cap to the glorious summit, the summation of my trip before it's back *home* for me. I struggle up the icy slope, thinking I could really slip and slide all the way off that cliff and die! But don't we feel most alive when we've cheated death? I think of Tyler Durden in *Fight Club* holding the pistol up to the pitiful convenient store worker's head, threatening his life. Why does he go to such an extreme? Because tomorrow his breakfast will taste better than it ever has before, because tomorrow he'll see a bright new world (the same world, but through clearer eyes). And any time I think about that scene, I think, *Palahniuk, you're a genius.*

I reach the top, the grey rock summit above the icy slope, and now I'm standing on the peak of New York thinking, "I can't wait 'til I conquer Everest!" And just as I'm kickin' myself for forgetting a camera, the man asks me if I want him to take my picture. He says he'll email it to me, so we snap each other's photos next to the Mt. Marcy info plaque, overlooking all the high peaks. I had hoped to read or write or at least meditate up at the top, but it's brisk up here. The wind whips through at 60 mph and my jeans have frozen solid from the knee down (where I had soaked them in the stream). I'm cold, yes, but I'm content for the seven mile walk back. And standing here, the highest person in New York, I feel a newly born inspiration, a mental boost that matriculates through body and soul as well! So after only five minutes at the summit, we're ready to head back down.

We talk about the wind. We talk about mountains and women and all sorts of tremendous things. He's still relatively young in his fifties, but he's lived his hair white like an old man. So the next three hours we walk together down the mountain talking about the outside world, and when we run out of things to say, we comment on where we are. He says things like, "oh, ya these mountains sure are beautiful," or "Hey, watch your step right here," simple lines to break a silence. I want him to poison me with words; I want him to say things like, "I'll tell you how the sun rose. A ribbon at a time." But he's simple, a genuine man and a caring man. And one time I slip on the ice bridge and fall at a bad angle, knee bending under me, my body falling backward off the side, and behind me he grimaces for me. But I'm alright and so we're back on our way to the lodge. Only about a mile from the lodge, I pick up my ruck sack where I left it, glad I found it and glad to see it not tampered with. Back in the parking lot it's only his car and one other, my truck is in another lot. So I guess here it's time to say goodbye. It feels weird to spend four hours up and down a mountain with a stranger telling him your deep seeded thoughts, then it feels weird to say goodbye so abruptly. But I leave him my email so he can send the pictures and we can keep in touch, but I know he'll probably forget.

And all this time I was floating on the wing of this man, his conversations occupied me and I forgot all about my misery, and I think to myself, if a conversation with somebody can do that, why can't I do that with my mind? Therein lies the power of the mind.

Oh and there he is, my good old American truck, just sitting there patiently waiting for me. There he is, my ride home, and I feel a new burst of glee, thinking how tonight I'll be home. Tonight I'll be in my own bed, on a full stomach, back with my RIT entourage! At this point, I don't even know why I'm still here. I've gotten what I came for, and now my next adventure

47

should be home. So I drive out of this rural seclusion and back toward civilization, stopping at the first restaurant I see. It's a Friendly's, and boy does it look friendly! Ode to vanilla milkshakes and honey-BBQ chicken strips! Chicken quesadillas for an appetizer and oh, why not a dessert to top it off! I sit alone in my filthy jeans, dirty up and down my arms and on my face, not showered in almost a week—what a sight I must be! (what a stench too!)

Happy on my new full belly, I drive next door to fill up on gas. I know Montreal is only an hour or so north, and I've never been to French Canada. Now that I don't have to worry about being hungry or lost or without shelter in the dangers of the wild, I consider touring the famous city for a day. Besides, it's the NHL playoffs, and I think Montreal is playing tonight. Hmm, nice comfortable bed or Montreal to watch the riots?? Montreal it is. Gotta experience everything, right?

So now I'm headed north instead of south on I-87, and only an hour later I'm driving through Canada and headed to the outskirts of Montreal for a nice cold beer and some hot chicken wings to watch the game. I pull into a parking lot at the end of a long village row, little shops and taverns that once looked so pretty until the crooks moved in and the good people moved out. Now it carries the beaten Romance of a college town where the kids abuse the unappreciated Victorian beauty. And the worst part: this Romantic old village, now a rundown rendezvous for old drunks and young alcoholics, is going to host riots tonight, win or lose for Montreal. So I get out of the truck and smoke as I walk all along the cobblestone—the lonely drifter I am, shoulders rounded and head hunched, hands in my coat pockets as I waltz down these desolate rows, stoned and looking only so far ahead as my next step. To me, right now, nothing matters. It's a sort of sadness where I'm not really sad anymore, just tired. I think about her, and how we were supposed to have dinner the night before I left. She was supposed to be my last company, the girl in my thoughts, the spirit of my thoughts. And even *she* blew me off. I think about how I had dressed myself all up, how I had planned the entire night, and how she blew me off like it was a fucking joke to her. And I remember walking the lonely paths of RIT, alone in the rain, smoking and drinking my scotch from the bottle until I had reached that point beyond sadness, no longer pissed off; I reached this point where all I could do was scowl contentedly. I miss the heavy drunkenness.

I miss the grip of the drink.
Remember me in that old dark room?
Afternoons with the shades drawn
To give
The room
That dim lit glow, that melancholy sick.
And I would wake—too late, too late
But stumble out of the top bunk, and hit my head
Or scrape my shin, I always did.
Reach for the bottle and catch a whiff,
It always sent me running for the sink.
I was a mess, and you never even knew.
Where were you all this time, huh?
You had your wine, I had my scotch,
You had your dreams and I? my tragedies.
Poor me. But hello drink. Sting my tender heart,
All the way down, one gulp, then two and three
But four—
Vomit.
Wipe your mouth, you sad young man.
It was always a scribble at the
Keyboard.

I got distracted easily, alcohol makes me horny.
But my girl was never around.
I didn't have a girl.
I didn't have a girl.
And I still don't.
I've never had a girlfriend. I've loved twice.
And now I don't have my drink.
I prefer it this way.
Smile, pretty girl.

I think of *Samudaya* with an arrogant cynicism, and duck into the shabbiest tavern in the whole strip. Inside I order a beer and start scribbling lines on a napkin. "We walk through the days like stoned shadows, but under midnight's blanket, where shadows are extinct, we cry out. These are the prolific hours. While everyone sleeps and I am up and jogging in a mind marathon. We stand aside, observant, cool. We scowl under sharp brows at the passing people. We watch them exist their waste. And we pity them for never questioning it. We scowl, yes, but we scowl content, for we have sought the answers. And through judgmental eyes we see an ignorant society living a life they have been duped into thinking is worthwhile. Obligations, deadlines, hollow promises—because truth has been lost. It is only when one can renounce all fiction that he can begin to seek truth. In order to relinquish himself from the strangle of lies, he has to redefine his ambitions. Enlightenment, nirvana yields him truth. But people are ungrateful, they overlook their importance. Truth exists only beyond the superficial. Will you ever **know**?" And when I write "know" I press too hard and tear the napkin.

I order chicken wings and the puck drops for the start of the game. Here I am in this dingy, dank place. Old gamblers and truck drivers talking

French in the corner, it's *le* hockey and poker games for them, and all I can think about is solitaire. And if it were my friends over there in the corner, they'd be talking beer pong and rosary or fine wine and dancing words. Oh, I'm so out of place in this French land, but I can't see myself anywhere else at the moment. And that's the true sadness, the real life misery that I can't seem to escape. There is no reason, but why? I'll ask myself this all my life and just keep running around in circles. And here I am, some prick kid in a bar writing about *nirvana* on ripped napkins thinking he's on some sort of path to enlightenment or truth. But all I am is an ambiguous pile of words and ramblings, just as fucked up as every other kid my age. I'm nothing special, and the only thing my napkin says is just how ordinary I really am. So I drink my beer in quietude, eating my wings and enjoying the game like a normal person, happy to be fed and drunk and stoned.

As the game goes on, I start to get into it, caught up in all the French hullabaloo, the jeers and cheers from the now packed bar. It's a magnificent game really, the fast pace action, the barbaric checking and graceful maneuvering, there's strategy and speed and hitting and fighting and adrenaline! And as the rivalry begins to turn from heated to hostile, two big guys start goin' at it on the ice. I mean, grabbin' each other at the collar and hammering fists into each other's faces, neither one going to be the first to drop. And anybody who's ever been in that raging, adrenaline pumping situation knows that neither of these guys even feel a thing right now (but, oh tomorrow they'll feel it!). They say fighting is barbaric ignorance, that hockey is no better than the Romans and their gladiators. Pshhh, except that hockey isn't exactly watching people get eaten by tigers. Yes, we shouldn't fight. But fighting is a product of passion and pride and principle. Without competitive passion and pride, we would have no motivation to strive to better ourselves. And without a fight now and then to test ourselves, we are only denying our abilities, living in a lying bubble, afraid to face the world. Fighting is an inevitable and necessary part of life. (Now, I'm not talking about frat party brawls and drunken douchebaggery. And I'm not justifying war or violence either.) Recognize that people are better at different things, some are strong in mind, and others are strong in body. Either way, we will never live up to our potential if we never have to fight (physically *and* mentally) to prove ourselves. Yet they take away our dodgeball in gym class because it "picks on the weak." Yeah, so let's take away all incentive for the "weak" to get any stronger or tougher by working hard to fight back. Instead, let's lie to them and let them live fairy tale lives. That way, when they get a job in the real world, they'll expect everything to be handed to them, and they'll just crash and burn. Great logic, pussies. Yes, without that primitive drive to prove ourselves worthy or better, we become slugs, sleeping our days away and passing through life with no great ambition, no dynamic. And oh what a tragedy to let a life go to waste! Now tell me sports aren't great; tell me blood, sweat, and tears aren't *natural!*

The hockey game is close and every time the Flyers bring the puck down to the Canadians goal, the French men in the bar go *nuts!* And even I get caught up, yelling "FUCK" when Montreal misses a shot, or "beat his ass!" during fights. It's a lively place, no longer that run-down hovel it was from the street. And the clock is counting down 10…9…8… and Montreal is down 3-2 with one last break away, he's skatin' fast, past one defender, he passes it back…the one timer at the clock!

He misses. Montreal loses and the French men are on a rampage, smashing beer bottles and storming the streets. I tell you, hockey in Montreal is like no sport in America. Out in the streets, die-hards are raging. They're fighting and smashing beer bottles and flipping cars! Now this is a scene! Everyone is cursing their drunken French, and here I am, the lone American, walking the cobblestone path all nonchalantly, hands in my pockets, smirk on my face, just watchin' the scene play out in front of me. The cops have already set up road blocks at each end of the street, and riot control, with their electric shields and big bubble helmets are coursing together, eager to club and stun any debauchers. So here I'm leaning back, one foot on the wall and my hands in my pockets when some French policeman starts stabbing questions at me. "Huh? I speak English." I tell him.

"Do you have identification?" he asks.

"No."

"Where are you from?"

"America."

"Where is your passport?"

"I don't have one."

"Put your hands against the wall and spread your legs!" he orders.

"What? I'm not doing anything. Don't you have other people to worry about? I'm not doing anything wrong!" I tell him.

"At this point we are placing you under arrest. You have the right to remain silent…yatta yatta yatta." Great, I went and got myself fuckin' arrested in French Canada. I'm in the back of a cop car, hands cuffed behind my back like I'm some sort of *criminal* and all I wanted to do was see the city for a day and go *home!* That's French fucking Canada for you.

So they haul me away from that black and white street with its blazing orange infernos under a red and blue siren ('cause I guess I'm that dangerous) to St. Jean where they throw me in jail. Can I just say: this is not what I had planned for this adventure. In jail, it's a whole mess of Montreal fans and meth fiends—grimy French people with rotting teeth and contagious sores. I'm in a room being searched and stripped of my hoodie and shoes, and after the typical "name-birthdate-address" questions (I tell them I'm homeless and they look at me like they think I'm lying) they throw me in a single cell. There is a metal toilet, a concrete slab with a thin mattress on it, a high ceiling with obnoxiously bright fluorescent lighting that reflects blindingly off the white walls, and it's just not warm enough, that torturing temperature where it's almost warm enough, but it just isn't and it just won't ever be. On the mat are two blankets, 4'x5' and not even long enough to cover my feet. No pillow, so I use one folded blanket as a pillow. It's gotta be one a.m. by now, and I'm wondering when they're gonna turn off this fucking light. They don't. They never do. But somehow I manage to doze off a bit. At least until five in the morning when some cracked out skank starts running her mouth. Picture your stereotypical crack whore: scraggly, unwashed hair, itching and twitching up and down her arms, popping, bloodshot eyes…that's her. Her squealing is all in French, but trash sounds the same in any language. She's bitching and swearing about whatever she's in for, and I just want to tell this crazy bitch to shut her yapping so I can get some sleep. I want to tell her that a lot of people have had it worse than she does (she looks like she's guilty anyway, if not of the crime she's been arrested for, she's guilty of something!) Finally after an hour of her banging on her metal door and howling like a deranged banshee, I get up and walk to the door yelling, "SHUT THE FUCK UP YOU NEUROTIC WHORE!" I know, I know, it's not exactly Zen-like, but I'm at my wits end. Scratch that, I was at my wits end yesterday after Mt. Marcy. Add not just a straw to the camel's back, but an entire bale of worry (having been ARRESTED and all). My camel isn't suffering a fractured back, no. My camel is on his death bed coughing up his liver. My camel is in a full body cast, paralyzed from the lips down.

Z

And at seven a.m., the room still glowing alight, the guards slide two pieces of toast and a cup of java under my door. At nine a.m. the guard opens my door and calls for me to go with him. I pocket the toast and think about spilling the coffee just to make their lives that much harder, but it wouldn't do anything but add unnecessary fuel to the fire. Back at the search room, they return my hoodie and shoes and I'm introduced to two new detectives (like Canadian FBI agents) who will take me to court. The one, Elliot, is a stout man who wears chic glasses and a dark suit. The other, Roger, is an old grumpy man, white hair and a foul mouth. Both speak English well, and both seem like pretty good guys. "You ready to go? It's gonna be a long day for you!" Elliot tells me.

On the way to the courthouse, Elliot tells me that I might get banned from Canada forever. If I weren't so strung out and worrying right now, I'd probably laugh. Banned from Canada, hah. That's practically an accomplishment!

Roger's on the phone, and the one side of his conversation I hear doesn't sound too pleasant. "Well, why the fuck would they tell us not to do it like that? I can't deal with this shit anymore!"

Elliot leans back and tells me he's retiring at the end of the month. Roger hangs up and starts muttering something to Elliot, "These people are fuckin' retarded! Only a few more weeks of this bullshit and I'm out!" He's that always angry cop character you see in movies, the unorthodox, old fashioned type who'd rather give the criminal a crack in the back of the head with the butt of his pistol. The type who likes to take justice into his own hands, and say it was in self-defense. He's the good type, and I like his spunk.

From the back seat I decide to change the subject. I say, "Shoot, if they're gonna kick me outta here, I better enjoy the drive. Could be the last time I pass through Canada!" Elliot and Roger laugh and we start talking like normal guys, no longer that awkward cop-prisoner "I'm better than you, 'cause you're a bad guy" stuff. We're cracking jokes and talking women, and the only difference is that I'm here in the back seat with my wrists cuffed behind my back.

We pull up to the courthouse, Roger going on about not being able to find decent parking. "I'm an old man, I've paid my dues! You'd think these bastards would let us park up front!" We get out and walk in, Elliot in front, badge out flashing all official like, and Roger behind me. I walk in like some kind of delinquent, hands still cuffed behind me. I'm thinking, you know besides all the shitty stuff like having a record and maybe going to jail, this is kinda cool. Chicks dig the bad boys, right? French chicks are no different. I walk in with a cocky smirk, fantasizing about hooking up with some hot French girl. She's on her knees and saying, "Oh, poor bahby! Let me give you blow job before you get locked up," in her erotic accent. Inside are a bunch of high school-college aged kids, a group of 'em, like they're on a field trip to see the bad guys or something. The girls turn their heads, trying to be inconspicuous with their double takes, but they're checking me out, the "bad boy, he don't take nothin' from nobody!" Hah. Me and my fantasies.

So now we're waiting for a lawyer or something, who was supposed to be here an hour ago. Eh, I'm in no hurry. Two men who work at the border walk in and introduce themselves as Carl and Arthur. Both are nice and act normal, none of that elitist attitude with them either. Arthur is soft spoken, a kind and gentle mien. Carl is also very helpful. He gives me his card telling me I can call him if I need anything (though I don't know what I might need him for). We're still waiting on that lawyer and now it's lunch time. Elliot and Roger are pissed the guy isn't here yet, so they say, "Fuck him, we're going to lunch. You hungry?"

We go out to the car, and they ask me what I want to eat, and I'm thinking, what is this? First class arrested? They decide we'll go to a place called *Le Coq Rapide* or something. The Rapid Rooster. "Kids around here call it the quick dick," Roger tells me. It's a chicken place, kind of fast food, but you sit down and there are servers. So right now it looks to me like I'm eating lunch on the Canadian Government's dollar. I order soup and a half chicken with mashed potatoes. The food is shitty, but what can I expect? Peter Gyres'?

"Did you guys see the hockey game?" I ask.

"What a heartbreaker, eh? We lost 3-2 and the guy hit the post right at the end!"

We talk hockey for a bit. Roger used to play semi-pro, and he tells us, "Don't worry, we'll come back to win it Saturday." He tells us all the little details of hockey that I never knew about. "I remember one game we played on soft ice, and our coach told us not to sharpen our skates the night before. Well, the other team did, and they were slipping all over the ice. Much better team than we were, but we won 'cause our coach knew how to play the ice."

Elliot tells us about a new girl he took out a few nights ago, "Oh, I think I'm in love," he says with puppy eyes. It's hard to believe I have to go back to court, then to prison or whatever they decide to do with me. We finish up our lunches (it was on the Canadian Government's dollar, ha!) and head outside. Turning out of the parking lot is a tiny, bright yellow chicken car, and I turn to Elliot and say, "What is that? The Cock Mobile?"

We drive back to the courthouse, and Elliot and Roger don't even bother to cuff me. "You're not gonna run off on us, are you?" Roger asks.

Back inside the courthouse we're still waiting. Roger's bored and starts talking to me, asking me about what I do. I tell him what I had been doing, about wandering toward the east coast to hop a freight ship and wander the world for a year. I tell him about my other adventures, how I had wanted to write a book. I say I'm not a bad kid, that I was either going to West Point come summer, or wandering the globe then climbing Mt. Everest in the spring.

He's probably used to dealing with the typical criminal type, but he gets the impression that I'm not such a bad guy after all. "Well, it sounds like you've got a good head on your shoulders, kid. Hopefully all of this will pass. And take it from an old guy; don't let those dreams slip away. Before you know it, you'll be too old like me, looking back and wondering why you didn't take more chances." I find wisdom everywhere.

Well, the lawyer finally decides to show up, it was the prosecutor we were waiting on, no less. He's got the look of a successful bachelor, in his fifties, good-looking, and smart too. Probably drives a Cadillac and lives in a hip pad (hip for a guy in his fifties, I mean). Elliot and Roger talk to him first to go over logistics and to paint my image for this guy who's prosecuting me; they tell him I'm a good person, not dangerous or insolent. Next, I meet my lawyer…Miss Gail. Oh, Miss Gail. She's *gorgeous!* Or smokin' hot depending on how you look at it—and smart! We talk in a room about what is going to happen, we talk about my options. She speaks English well in her seducing accent, and I want her bad.

I have to wait in the lobby while the lawyers go at it, trying to settle the case out of court. I just want to go *home* but it looks like the only place I'm going is prison. Already, I'm playing it out in my head. I'm thinking, "If anyone pulls shit with me, I'm gonna go down swingin'!" I'm thinking prison is gonna be like you see in movies. I'm not scared, exactly. Apprehensive I guess is a better word for it.

Miss Gail calls me back into the room and tells me what will probably happen. She tells me what bail will cost, and I tell her I can't afford it. I tell her I'll just do my time, not like I have anything better to do. I dropped out of

RIT for the third quarter (for reasons). I had planned on either going to West Point or wandering the world, writing a book, doing volunteer work, and climbing Everest for the next year. None of my credits from RIT would transfer, and I would be starting as a freshman again anyway, so why waste the 10 weeks and $4000 dollars. I dropped out (and of course, my family didn't see it the way I did. To them, I was a drop out. Period. They couldn't see past the *label*, they couldn't see the justifications. I didn't care, I was doing what I thought was right for me at the time. It's the way I've always tried to live, just doing the right thing.) Well, now it looks like I'll be spending third quarter in prison. But I stand by what I'm doing, I've done nothing unethical and I'm not hurting or burdening anybody. I said I would do something, and I did it, no empty words, no pretenses, no hollow promises. I'm not cowering behind lies; rather, I'm exposing truth—a renouncement of fiction.

I walk down the aisle into the court room. Miss Gail tells me the judge is in a good mood today, "so cooperate." The hearing is in French and broken English, but I trust Miss Gail, and she queues me on what to do and say. The judge says something and snaps his gavel, as if to seal my fate. I glance back at Elliot who's watching me with sorry eyes as he hands my wallet to Miss Gail. Two guards walk up behind me and grab me at each arm to take me away, and suddenly everything is so surreal. My mind is drifting confused, as if it's finally hitting me that I'm really being sent to prison...*me!*

They handcuff me in the courtroom and I'm escorted behind those ominous doors that separate the condemned from freedom; the doors you see in movies or in shows like *Law and Order*. Like most, I never dreamed I would pass through them; it is the portal for the wicked and evil, to thrust them into a hyper-reality where primordial beasts are tamed until they are seen fit to re-enter society. But here I go, cuffed at the wrists and ankles as though I pose such a ferocious threat. With the deep and hollow echo of the doors closing behind me, my head begins to ring, and I realize that sound is the cessation of my freedom. I am in a cage, to be locked away from society.

I'm shuffled into an elevator; sectioned off by Plexiglas is a small compartment so the animal won't bite the guards—just put a fucking muzzle on me and teach me to play dead. We take the elevator two floors closer to hell where I am pulled and prodded into a cell to be detained until they're ready for inspection. It's a big, empty room, clearly made to house several inmates, but I'm the only one in it now. And that's how I wish it would stay. The walls are decorated with an array of scratchings and scrapings, nobodies leaving their mark, anticipating the day their fantasies of fame and fortune come true. It is a marking of territory, a bold claim that they'll never live up to. They're no-good criminals, and now, so am I. I take a seat on the cold metal bench; I haven't showered in six days, my hair slicks itself pretty with a natural gel of grime, my face is coated in the grit accumulated from surviving the Adirondack Mountains the week before. I sit contented, alone and in silence. I know what lies ahead of me, but for some reason I'm ok with that. I think back to the richness of the mountains, the upturned trunks that expose a spider web of rooting, rabbit holes that no doubt lead to a wonderland of some sort. But it is hard to imagine a land more wondrous than those serene mountains. And to think, just yesterday I sat meditating atop the icy peak of Mount Marcy; I was the highest person in New York.

But for every high you'll hit that low, they say. And here I sit.

The Guards call me out for the routine frisking. I'm stripped ass naked and checked thoroughly, the entire time wondering if the prison has a decent library. So I throw my clothes back on and they slap on cuffs, and then it's a solemn walk to another cage. But this time I've got cell mates, three of them. One is calm, he's wearing a Montreal Canadians jersey, and he keeps to himself mostly. The other two make me cringe for what might await me at the joint.

Two crack heads lie feet to feet on the metal benches. The one, showing the sad symptoms of withdrawal, is hypersensitive. He incessantly scratches and vigorously kneads his arms, neck, and body. His ankles cross and re-cross, never finding a comfortable position. Each time he shuffles and twitches, his ankle cuffs clank obnoxiously on the metal bench. His unkempt, blonde hair hangs shoulder length in greasy strands that stripe his face, and through his stringy hair, a scared eye watches me walk in, as though he were a fragile animal. My guess is this guy's fried his brain stupid; I've talked to smarter dogs. He coughs deep from tar-coated lungs and hocks up a throat full of mucus and crack residue. Disgusting. Through his wheezing mouth I notice the rotting teeth. One incisor hangs desperately. Another tooth a few spots over hangs, too—sick teeth that groan and shiver with every diseased cough. It's as though these teeth have been afflicted with the cancer of his thousands of cigarettes before his lungs will get the chance. His teeth are terminal cases, and I could say the same about him.

He wipes his face with heavy palms like a toddler, no grace or dexterity. Now he's wiping the grease from his face on his stained white t-shirt so vigorously that he continues to stretch it out at the collar. It's clear this shirt has been worn for several days straight. It's clear, also, that his grey denim pants haven't been changed. I decide to name him "Crackhead."

The other guy lies sluggishly on the bench and lifts only his head when I enter. A doofy looking head, too wide at the top, or too narrow at the chin maybe. His dumbstruck expression is made even dumber by his haircut. Shaved around the sides, long on the top, and faded like idiot hair. Picture a bowl cut, but awkwardly angled, I guess. Something about it bothers me.

"*J'no ce quoi?*" or some French shit, he says to me.

"Huh?" I grunt, unenthusiastically, the last thing I want to do is talk to these fleas.

"Ahh, English?"

"American," I retort, sharply.

"Ah, American! What you are here for, dude?" He's using me as an opportunity to practice his mediocre English, and I don't like it. But I'm headed to prison and I'm not about to start unnecessary trouble.

I tell him what I'm in for, and he nods with a stupid grin, flashing more diseased teeth. His teeth are holocaust victims, bent and broken, but lined array. They are tiny and decrepit, like dying old men. Yellow or grey or green, and dirty. His incisors are small and sharp looking, either chipped or eroding as though his saliva is acidic, something corrosive. I wouldn't doubt it. I watch him tongue his sickly teeth, running that worm in his mouth between the gaps and across pointed tips, it's a mindless habit for him, and I know he doesn't even realize he's doing it. He introduces himself as "Norman" I think, or something like it—tells me he's in for "trafficking...long time."

He rubs his right thumb with his left hand, and I notice his right thumb is scarred up. It looks like it was nearly sliced off, but sewn back on. It's stiff, and I'm guessing the nerve damage has left it tingling to the touch, and Norman has grown to like the tickle. He perches himself up on the bench with a startling jump of energy, resembling a long type of bird. Norman is probably six foot two and relatively skinny. His spine bends as he brings his knees to his chest, perched on the metal bench, neck hung low in defeat.

I'm not keen on sitting down; I just stand in the corner. The Montreal fan paces slowly in a small circle, Norman sits perched, and Crackhead is now up and twitching, itching, as though there is something to do but nowhere to go. The three of them talk French, jokes I suppose, because they chuckle together. Crackhead has a booming and happy laugh, but not an innocent one. It's a laugh that exposes a delinquent life.

Across the hall, in another cell, is a single man. Groomed with short, dark hair and an eerie goatee, he looks like a David. I glance at him wondering why he is alone. *Could he be some twisted murderer? A serial killer?* I'm nineteen and lost in a world I don't belong in, my imagination is not my friend.

The guards open a slot about two feet from the ground and Norman pounces down from his perch. He knows exactly what to do, it's clear he's been here before. The slot is for us prisoners to stick our hands through so the guards can throw the chains back on our wrists. We rank up and once we're cuffed, the guards open the door. The four of us are marched back to that first cell I was put in, along with two other guys: David and a third meth head, call him...Speedy. I put a "don't fuck with me" glare on and scowl my brow. I'm

65

trying to look bad ass, but Speedy is the real deal, and I don't think he's the least bit threatened.

Speedy is a loquacious and belligerent fella. He's obviously poor, but wearing an expensive "gangsta" hoodie and ghetto jeans that don't match. He walks with a bounce and lean on one side, a strut that says, "I don't give a fuuuck, man!" He wears a smile that flashes more dull and rotted teeth, but he wears it shamelessly. He looks like he is forty years old, and acts like he's eighteen. He's cool in a dirty crack addict sort of way. From this cell, we're taken down a steel ramp, our ankle chains echo impersonally off the metal. A van waits to deliver us like commodities to Sorel, where the prison is. The guards offer us cigarettes; I refuse one, but the rest of them snatch 'em up. I would be bathed in cigarette smoke for the duration of the van ride, and then the duration of my sentence.

The ride was an hour spent listening to these French bastards snort and howl at their own juvenile and, no doubt, vile jokes.
They were loud and rude, but they didn't bother me. David spoke English pretty well, and helped translate to the rest of them why I was in and where I was from. Speedy knew some English too, and when he heard I was American, he nodded, pleased.

Turning to me he said, "Ahh, American eh?! Like the Bloods and the Cripps. BANG BANG! HA!" he roared, imitating a shootout, that notorious gangsta life that Speedy idolized.

I carried on casual conversation with them when they had questions. Through the cage in the back window, David would spot a pretty girl driving and yell, "ELLO, BAHBY!" We would all stand up and stare and shout like wild beasts at the potential mate. I found this funny and oh so predictable, so I even joined in and cracked a smile. Speedy was crazy, and I made it a point to stay on his good side. He told me he was in for possession of a gram of cocaine and a shit load of speed. He also told me, though he didn't have to, that this was not his first trip to Sorel.

I've started to open up a bit, David and Speedy joke around with me. They know it's my first time, and they assure me it won't be too bad. They say they'll take care of me. Speedy even tells me, "Hey, man, I take care of you. We roll some joints, you know. You hang out with me we smoke some joints, man! HAHA-HAHA-HA!" I can't tell if he's kidding, but if he isn't, I dare not think of how they get the stuff into prison.

We arrive in Sorel and we're taken to the "bullpen." It is a room that will hold about ten people. It has a picnic type table, one solid piece of metal painted blue. And there's a toilet, also one solid piece of metal. Twenty minutes later, the guards return to the bullpen to take the cuffs off, ankles and hands. We're taken, one by one, into the next room. I'm in no rush, so I am the last to go. In the room, I am stripped down and searched again.

I give them my name, but when they ask for my address, I tell them I'm homeless. This raises their brow; they think I'm fucking with them. I explain that I just came from the Adirondacks, that I had been living off the land for the past week and that I had been wandering the globe, aimlessly yet for very definite purposes. They're puzzled, I hate when dumb people think they're smarter than me.

That's when I ask the English speaking guard if there's a decent library at the prison. He nods and points for me to line up for a mug shot. I fluff my hair and stick my unshaven chin out strong and tough-like. I've come to peace with the fact that I've been arrested, and that I have prison to look forward to, I'm gonna make a story out of it! Click.

They give me a rolled up blanket with sheets and a towel, and a little goodie bag: soap, razor, toothbrush.

Out in the hall I meet up with the other guys again, we're locked between doors, waiting to be herded to our designated wings like cattle. Smoking isn't allowed, but they light up a cigarette anyway. *What are they gonna do? Throw 'em in jail?*

I'm praying I don't get stuck with Crackhead or Norman. They look like they're itching with disease. Speedy is dirty too, but he seems to have connections and he likes me. The Montreal fan is quiet and considerably less dirty than the crack heads, though still less than pleasant (not that I'm so great myself, I ain't showered in six long days). David would be cool though.

Well, David, Norman, and the Montreal fan are taken to wings A and B on the first floor, the rest of us are marched up stairs to C and D. I'm put in C-wing with Crackhead (ugh) and Speedy. Speedy walks in like he owns the place, slappin' old friends up and crackin' jokes already. Crackhead sticks behind Speedy, like a timid bitch. I walk in, modest but with a confident affect about me. The wing is crawling with more grime. More crack fiends, murderers, thieves, and all around shady characters. The biggest and baddest looking of them all sits on an upside down bucket; he's taken to building models with popsicle sticks, and oh, is he fantastic at it! Here sits this bear of a man (I call him the Bear in my head), grizzly beard and sheared, wild looking hair. Tattoos adorn beefy arms and a puffed out chest—thick thighs that carry around a sizeable gut. His eyes are narrow—piercing and impersonal. A scar—stab wound—keloids diagonally across his chest, and just under it, across his heart, is his most precious tattoo. Written in a child's writing is the name "Audrey" and her drawn heart. A note written for her daddy before he would be taken from her for so long he wouldn't recognize her the next time he saw her. The tattoo turns my heart, and I feel a sense of compassion toward this peaceful beast.

He says something to me in French. I have to shrug and tell him I don't understand. He simply points to my blanket, then to the window ledge. I can put my stuff down and take a seat. I leave my blanket near those magnificent popsicle stick models as the guards yell for me, Crackhead, and Speedy to grab a dinner tray.

Dinner is welcome, as it's the first full meal I've had in a week. Some noodles sloshed in a sort of grey gruel sauce. A dessert cup with some brown shit inside, burned around the edges. And a pint of milk to drink. The guard tells me to keep my silverware; I don't get another set until dinner the next day. The pasta is tasteless, the sauce: bland, but I scarf it down like I haven't eaten much in a week (oh, wait…I haven't). I take a bite of "turd-in-a-cup" and choke it down. The stuff is putrid and I ask if anyone wants it. No takers. Surprise.

I slide the tray under the door and rinse my silverware. I have nothing to do now but watch French TV. Fuck me.

Two hours of *"j'ue quoi pas cio"* shit later and the guards are back to take me and Crackhead back to the bullpen. Somehow Speedy scored himself a cell in the wing. At this point I'm just too tired to think or do anything. I get up methodically, grab my roll, and follow the guards back down stairs, back to that same bullpen we were corralled into earlier that night.

We're given thin mats and pillows that must have six strains of disease woven between the fabric, but with our sheets is a pillow case, need I say I'm grateful for at least that? I lay the mat out and fix my sheets, then lie down exhausted. There are some new faces in there with me, and one of them strikes up nostalgic conversation with Crackhead. He's another dirty bastard, more violent looking too. They suck at cigarettes like desperate piglets at a nipple: tobacco nourishment, good for the bones!

The two of them talk exuberantly without discretion, apathetic or oblivious to the fact that other people are trying to sleep. The prison guards so kindly leave the fucking lights on, which doesn't help much. The two disease-bags chatter like school girls (though I'd guess the topics of discussion differ slightly) until one in the fucking morning. And when they finally lie down, the dude at my foot starts snoring. I stare; awake, at closed eyelids –faux sleep– reminiscent of my insomniac days during last miserable summer.

Prison life: I left my sympathy on the outside.

8

The next day we're awoken by the guards banging their sticks on the barred doors. This is annoying, and I am less than pleased.

It's seven in the morning, and I've been hovering in that half-sleep, half-awake state all night. Somewhere between the French slurring, irritating snoring, and disgusting flatulence, I failed to fall asleep. But now it's morning and I'm again reminded of why I hate these assholes.

We're handed tin trays with milk, Rice Krispies, and two pieces of toast. Prisoners are crafty little buggers, quite capable of utilizing everything around them. The milk cartons can be opened up, the cereal can be dumped in, and *vuala*, you have yourself a bowl of cereal.

I watch Norman struggle with his milk carton, the thumb on his right hand hanging, useless. He takes a bite of toast, flashing that million dollar grin of his, and I near lose my appetite. Those small sharp teeth cut and shear into the toast easily, but even toast seems too solid a food. I'm expecting those victimized teeth to fall right out of his face with every bite, dead. His stupid hair is knotted in the back now, having just woken up, and the mildly delirious expression smeared across his aging face gives him that always-confused look, a look that would sound like "derrr…"

Crackhead sits himself across the table. I get the impression that he is afraid to make eye contact with me, he looks down and away like a scared puppy, searching for an excuse to not acknowledge me. I don't care, though, I prefer it this way.

He sets his tray down and starts scratching and itching his arms and neck, fucking crack heads. I watched the kid wake up and immediately start searching with heavy eyelids. I watched him find what he was looking for, his pack of cigs, and immediately he and his childhood friend light some up. Seven in the god damn morning and these addicts are sucking ash already. He, too, gives off the impression that he doesn't regularly brush his teeth, and I involuntarily shudder thinking of what creeps and crawls around his tongue and teeth. The good news: whatever it is, it probably has cancer by now and is on its way back to hell. Another fella bums a cig off Crackhead, I'm surprised by his generosity in giving the guy one, didn't hardly hesitate.

This guy is a truck driver, mid forties I'd say, and…he's got rotten teeth too, and a bushy mustache over a school boy grin. He belongs in jail, but he's not a popular type. Picture the kid in high school who would be so excited to be involved in a cool kid's conversation that he couldn't suppress a goofy smile. But as soon as his part in the story was over, he was exempt from the group, that flicker of hope extinguished one more time. This fella was that kid, always eager to be included, but he never was unless he served a temporary purpose. He's harmless, at least emotionally. I wish I could say the same about his hygiene. He too sucks back a stick of tobacco before a coffee breakfast. Healthy, right?

At this point I'm getting pissed off again, and I can feel my blood pressure rising steadily. I decide to ignore the grime and scum around me and concentrate on my happy bowl of cereal breakfast. Just seeing the box of Rice Krispies is a boost in moral—the nostalgic blue with Snap, Crackle, and Pop. I listen to my cereal repeat those names like lost echoes of a youth so splendid, and now I'm feeling homesick. I want to be back with my friends, my family. I want to be back in Building 30 playing Halo with Corey, Kwamster, and Gimli. And Rob! HD *waka-waka!* I miss those nights when we were up to no good. Oh, how I miss the carelessness of those beloved nights! I had no responsibility, no worries. I was clean, full, and *happy!* I miss pretending to understand James Joyce's *Ulysses* and talking smart with Ian. Even Rigo's boisterousness would be so welcome, I would jump into his arms right now if I heard his *"que pasa amigos!"* Those times passed too quickly and now they're gone for a while. And here I sit cursing myself for taking them for granted. I wish Gimli would walk through that door and say, "Strap-on!" I wish he would tell me this is all a joke. I'm wondering what they must be thinking. *"I bet he's eating squirrels right now. I wonder if he's sucking off some trucker for a ride to the coast. He's probably back at the playboy mansion laughing at us right now! hahaha,"* they laugh, hoping the best for me, but joking the worst. Well, this is not the best, quite the opposite of my spring break journey. I know they've fucked with my computer already, I

74

know that detail was taken care of two hours after I left (dammit Corey!). I never thought I'd say this, but Keven, here it is, in writing: I MISS MEATSPIN! Oh, what I wouldn't give to walk into my laptop with that glorious spinning meat that has burned my eyes so many times before!

We're meandering through the bowels of the prison now, returning the mats and pillows. They take us to our respective wings and it's back to that smoke bath again. It's quiet when I walk in; most of the guys are still asleep. I take a seat at the table and tune in to some French TV. I still haven't seen a library, and now I really wish I could.

It's nine o'clock and the guy sitting next to me is puffing on his third hand rolled cigarette. He looks old and rough, faded tattoos around his thick arms. He's probably younger than my mother, but his lifestyle has clearly aged him considerably. He speaks only French, so he doesn't talk to me.

The time drags on and more people begin to wake, which means more people begin to smoke, which means the probability that I have a malignant, cancerous tumor growing in my lungs is steadily increasing. Thank you French Canada. Bear is awake and walking around in his underwear. As he passes, the others pat him on the back and say good morning. He's clearly well respected, and I wish I could know why. He doesn't smoke, and that seems to give him an uncanny wisdom in my eyes. I see him as rough and tough, but intelligent and deep too. He has been humbled by love (his Audrey), and he smiles contentedly as he concentrates on those popsicle stick models. He's the kind of man I would seek to talk to, if I understood French. But alas, the only French I know is a phrase taught to me by Speedy and David. *Sus ma beat!* Suck my dick.

And speaking of Speedy, here he comes, bouncin' down the hall with that cocky lean. He's cheery as can be; this is summer fun camp for him. And why shouldn't it be? Three hots and a cot, and he don't gotta work or nothin.' He's big man on campus around here, he knows everyone and he's with his best friends. That's the problem with this place. It's not rehabilitation; it's exacerbating the crime epidemic. I would hate to be a tax payer in Quebec, having to pay for these trash bags to eat and sleep warm while they sit around wasting needed labor, exchanging leisurely jokes and drug dealing knowledge. No, don't have the criminals who do nothing all day help Quebec out, let them waste honest citizens' tax dollars. And why don't you pay people overtime to work for the state. Yeah, that's logical, you French speaking fuck cases.

"Heyy, AmeriKAN!" Speedy says in his raspy accent. I smile back and nod my chin up like whatsup.

Now he's lightin' up a hand rolled one of his own and headed to the phone.

He's loud on the phone. It's in French, but I can guess he's talking to one of his homies. Loud cracks of laughter amidst his hollering into the phone end. He doesn't even hold it to his ear, just snaps lines into the speaking end. He's one of those eccentric people who talk with their bodies, as though he were talking to his buddy in person. He has that confident, even impudent affect about him, that demeanor that says, *"I don't give a fuuuck, man!"*

He's cool in that dirty, crack head sort of way.

Now I'm watching Shifty, a gaunt and sketchy looking man in a button-up light-blue shirt. The shirt hangs off his skeletal frame, he stands rounded at the shoulders, fine hair wispy and combed back. He talks with a nervous stutter and smokes fiendishly, but the tobacco is too weak to calm his nerves. He paces, strung out and anxious. He isn't a druggie like the other meth addicts, but he's antsy, always antsy for some reason. He kinda trips outta his cell, hands fumbling his pack of cigarettes. Finally he gets one out, sticks it in his lips, and leans his face over the toaster to light it on the red hot wire. He stands erect again, drawing in a soothing drag, relaxed for only a split second. The rough looking man on my left folds up the paper he's reading, stabs his cigarette butt into the tin tray, and stands up to confront Shifty. Shifty snaps out of his moment at ease with a nervous fright in his eyes. The rough man obviously has a problem with Shifty; he's in his face stabbing fingers in Shifty's chest with strong arms that once were young. His body language translates his staccato French for me. The rough man wears a tough frown under a scowled brow; he's slowly walking Shifty backward to a corner. Shifty has to duck his tall head under the TV shelf and now he's trapped. He stutters something nervously, an apologetic excuse. Bad choice. I see the rough man wind up and it's as though time has slowed, I know what's coming, Shifty does too as he contorts his face in anticipation, cigarette hanging from his lips. The rough man slaps a solid backhand across poor Shifty's face, slapping the cigarette sparking to the floor. Shifty's lips tremble as he awaits another in fear, but it doesn't come. The rough man backs off and gives Shifty a verbal threat, who then retreats back to his cell, his face lachrymose and terrified. The rough man assumes his position next to me and I'm scared something near shitless.

I'm nineteen years old and in a place I don't belong. I don't speak the language and I have only the slightest idea of prison etiquette—this hierarchical society based on physical dominance and violence. I ignore the rough man and keep quiet to myself. I glance at the smiling Speedy, still on the phone, as if to say, "I hope you got my back, man."

I'm nineteen years old in a place I don't belong; my imagination is not my friend.

The rest of the guys carry on like nothing happened. A mundane occurrence behind the bars of Sorel? I guess so.

The guards knock at the door and call for one of the inmates to pick up a bag of new clothes…and out of Speedy's cell strolls none other than Crackhead. His hair is a greasy ball of unkempt, his shirt is stained and stretched, but at least he's got a new one in the bag. He picks up his bag with a "*merci*" and waves the guards away, then catches Speedy's eye (who has since hung up) and slaps his hands together. His face lights up and he takes the bag back to Speedy's cell, Speedy in the lead. My guess is that's how the drugs get into the prison, and now Crackhead's scored some. I don't know if that's what it was for sure, and I'm not about to go check it out. You see, I've implemented an "avoid Crackhead at all times" policy.

An uneventful hour later, Crackhead pokes his grungy face out again, this time under a new hat that apparently came in the bag. It's one of those straight brimmed hats, a cool one I've never seen before, and he wears it backwards. This pisses me off, as he is anything but cool, and so dirty that his wearing this clean hat seems paradoxical and perturbs me. To my surprise, he's got a towel with him and he's headed to the shower. The shower is a single with a curtain. I was relieved to see this, as I had expected group showers and consequences to dropping the soap. Crackhead showers up and puts on less dirty clothes. To call them clean would be a trying euphemism, like calling fat girls "curvy."

And speaking of girls, damn I wish there were some. I haven't seen many girls in a week, and fantasies about my oh *so fine* lawyer still tease me. I remember hoping she would screw me over on the case, then feel bad and offer to make up for it in sexual favors, which I would have happily obliged to. That French accent, those porn star secretary glasses, boobs out to here, and a figure that could make Elton John hard; ooh! And couple that with her courtroom tenacity...what I wouldn't do for a night with her as my lover! Miss Gail would tease my dreams for years to come!

I think about her pressed up against me, me against her against the wall, her hand running down my belt line—that seductive tease in her eye. I want her in her skirt and suit, letting her hair loose of that prudent bun it's pulled back in. So I grab her at the waist and press my open lips to hers to find her soft tongue, hot and wet and oh so sweet. I want to be the one to tear that lawyer smock off her shoulders. I want to grab her at the waist and throw her one leg up on the chair, high heels and no stockings—bent over, back arched, head thrown back, her mouth open with the sexual thrill. I want her skirt up past her waist exposing her pink like animals in heat, because that's what I am; I'm a prisoner in a zoo. And I'm the one behind her slapping my thighs against her rich, creamy buttocks, sweat sticky and slapping loud—one hand grabbing at that thick dark hair and the other on those luscious breasts, tweaking at the nipple. I'm heavy on top and hitting it so hard I've got her pinned at the desk and just before I'm about to come I pull out and take her at the arm. But she can take me for an even wilder ride than I can fancy and she's already on her knees gobbing on me with such a crude appetite for sex—and when she pulls her head back to suck in air she's drooling her own taste, a gob of spit hanging from her full and puckered lips. I want her hot breath on me, I want her white lawyer shirt ripped at the buttons, those magnificent tits hanging out, skirt still up past her waist and she's going at me with that desperate desire of older women. The look that says "I'm way too experienced for you and I'm gonna do things to you you can't even imagine, kid." I want her, mouth and hands and tongue and cheek, workin' my cock 'til I'm weak at the knees—so I brace myself at the table and I'm about to go and when I do she's right there hungry for the load—I watch it drip down her chin, hot and wet and landing on the smooth skin of her chest. I watch it walk down the valley of her breasts and she's got that diabolical smile like my demon seed brings her that greedy satisfaction. We fuck like animals because that's all I am, caged up and forgotten.

Now I'm hard in a room full of dudes; embarrassed is an understatement. I consider masturbating to pass the time, letting my imagination run wild with fantasies of Miss Gail or the girls back home. I wish I could right now, it would be the most fun thing that's happened to me in the past few days! I left Rochester with an apathetic attitude, tired of people. I left Rochester with no one to orgasm to. But now I'm pretty sure I could rectify that problem! hah.

Lunch time arrives and we line up for our trays. It's a meat chunk and a scoop of mashed potatoes. For dessert: some sort of lemon pie shit. I grab my tray and head over to the juice. Hmm…red drink? or orange drink? I decide I'll try a small cup of each. Mistake. A guard rushes over like I just pulled a shank on someone, billy club raised to crack me in the skull. He tells me I can only get one drink. Fine, no need for the fucking club, asshole. He grabs the red cup and dumps it in the trash. I never understand this logic. He wastes the drink anyway; I could have just drunk it and remembered the one cup policy next meal time. But he's a dumb prison guard, and (perhaps more noteworthy) a fucking French Canadian…what do you expect?

The food is kind of tasteless, but I'm not complaining. In fact, I'm very much grateful for the food. Sure beats having to wake up to empty game traps or wet logs not conducive for a fire. I take a bite of the lemon shit and realize it's got a coconut topping. It's ok, but I'm not so keen on it. I toss the cup in the middle where it's up for grabs.

About one o'clock someone brings a box of books into the wing. The notion of books puts a bright smile on my face, and when I get up I see they're all in French. Fuck. I should have guessed so. I ask if there are English books and ten minutes later they bring some up. They're Reader's Digest books, three or four shortened stories in one, and they all suck. But I find one that catches my eye, *Escape to Honor*. It's a holocaust story of a German who escaped a concentration camp and joined the Ally forces to catalyze the Nazi defeat. The book has some other gay stories in it too, but I'm concerned with this heroic tale.

After about six pages, the guy who looks like a heavy metal maniac takes a seat next to me. I had seen him before, and at first glance, I was weary of this dude. Long straight hair down to his chest, tattoos up and down his arms, a calm but "I-could-kill-you-right-now-if-I-wanted-to" look on his face. Well, he sits next to me with a "What's up man."

He speaks English pretty well, and when I ask him about it, he says he grew up in Ontario. He's pretty fluently bilingual.

"So what are you in for, man?" he asks, mellow.

I give him the story and he gives me that "eh, what are you gonna do" look. I return the question and the conversation ensued as such:

"Attempted murder."

"Attempted murder? Must have been quite an extreme of emotion," said my dumb ass.

"Pshh, yeah. I dunno, I just snapped, man. My dad had his old friend over who used to beat us as kids. I shot up some heroin, drank a bottle of whisky and I just…I grabbed the knife and tried to fuckin' stab 'im man."

I had glorified the extremes of emotion; I had been so arrogant as to assert that I had experienced it all. And here sits this attempted murderer who humbles me beyond belief. I realize that I haven't experienced shit. I'm still a kid with just a tough life. And again I'm reminded of how grateful we should be to have grown up the way we have. Fuck, I mean…this guy's felt such a melancholy, such a violent rage that he's picked up a knife and plunged it through another living being with intentions to end that fucker's life! This is the real deal, none of this cry baby, oh poor me bullshit. Oh, the altered emotions, the murderous surge of diabolic adrenaline that must have been pumping through this man's heart, not to mention the heroin and whiskey. He was invincible at the time; he had a purpose and that was to end the man who would beat him as a kid. It is the definition of cold revenge, and I'm sitting next to the guy who did it, who experienced it.

"Wow…it'd make a good poem." I'm fucking stupid. *It'd make a good poem?* And that is the manifestation of my arrogance, my young and dumb self.

He just looks at me incredulously, "pshhh…a poem, man, shit." That was all he needed to say. I sat embarrassed and humbled in his presence. But it was this story that I so much needed. It was this hardcore story, in part, that brought about a change in my worldly philosophies. I know things, but I don't know it all, and neither do you!

He introduces himself as Stephen LeJour. "It means 'the day.' Le Jour in French, it means 'the day'." We make friends and talk about irrelevant stories to pass the time. We talk about watching English movies in French. We talk about Judge Judy and the show Cops.

The guards are at the door giving guys their prescribed medicine. Stephen gets a pill. "See this pill?" he says, holding it out in his palm. "It's the Cadillac of pills at this place. It's like Valium, but stronger—puts you on a cloud, man. Just sit back and float on the cloud."

We start talking about drug experiences. I'm curious about heroin and other opiates. I had never tried any, but I wanted to hear firsthand what they could do.

"It's incredible, like, you feel invincible or just amazing. Like think of your happiest moment and multiply it by a thousand."

We exchange stories about marijuana. He tells me about how he used to mellow out with it and Pink Floyd. I give him a talk on the benefits of the drug when used "responsibly." How it helped me to relax. How it taught me to open up and be comfortable with myself. I told him how it catalyzed a more confident and happier me. "Not that I need it to be happy or have a good time, but I did need to experience it in order to get to where I am today. It finished what alcohol started, but did it smarter." Then I tell him how a wise man challenged me to reach the same high through meditation. "I'm not there yet."

We talk about how marijuana affects one far less than alcohol.

"I mean, alcohol makes you violent and pissed off. Weed chills you out," he says.

"Yeah, exactly. It can help someone to be more comfortable with himself; it can work wonders and make you see the beauty in the world beyond a superficial level. It reveals a truer self."

I tell him about mushroom tales and psilocybin adventures—those long, so long nights that seem to last for ages and me and Brian would wander scene to scene, living and doing and thinking the worth of three days. I even tell him what I can remember of the poem I wrote: something about a psilocybin midnight, waves of triumphant emotion, and a shy shore laced with dream.

Stephen is more versed in opiates and hardcore drugs. He isn't one for the psychoactive stuff so much. I tell him how I first wanted to experience the psychoactive drugs to experience just how powerful our brain chemistry is. "So much lies in our subconscious. Think of dreams, think of how the mind can formulate these surreal scenes. There is so much more to the mind than what we know as reality, and psychoactive drugs are the key to this potentially enlightening vault. He tells me Salvia is also legal here in Canada, and I tell him about my salvia trip while sitting in my dorm room a few weeks prior.

"Madness. The world was on its head, gravity knew no stipulation. The rhythm and sequence of time was not to be interrupted. I had a sense of urgency to help some small creatures, cartoon-like in appearance, get on an amusement park ride, a roller coaster that launched into a spiraling tunnel just ahead. Behind me something was falling, or so I thought, off the edge of my desk, and I felt compelled to help it. There was another ride to my right too, three total. As I began to exit this strange and terrible hyper reality, my consciousness was thoroughly confused. I realized my speakers were playing music—Junkie XL, the song "Mushroom." I realized that the warping tunnel and amusement park rides were in fact the sound from the speakers, as though sound was not noise, but rather the atmosphere itself! There was no such thing as sound; it was the medium through which this world existed! I remember my spotter was sitting near me watching to make sure I was OK. Now jubilant at having experienced this, I rolled my chair over to him, startled to discover that every movement I made was predestined. And then came the paranoia. I was convinced that I was to be moving along a choreographed route, but I couldn't remember my steps. *What if I'm off-beat?!* With wide eyes and tightly rolled fingers I glanced back at the side of my desk, it carried a trippy green tinge, and the walls too were iridescently colored. I stood up and realized that the sound of the motor on the fan was pushing me backward. Yes, the sound, not the fan's blowing air. I told my spotter that I could let the sound take control, and I did. It wasn't overwhelming, just a light, steady push. It pushed me back to the door and I had to trudge back as though I were pushing up a steep incline, *but the room was flat!* I felt a hook descend from the hand of a faceless deity and snatch me by the lip, as though I were mere trout to some sort of divine superior. My pulse was high from anxiety and revelation. When I took a seat, I broke out in a cold sweat and realized that it was now turning into a bad trip. Luckily the ordeal ended after 20 minutes or so. I eased out of it, grateful for such a profound experience."

We're interrupted by the guards at the door. Apparently it was time to go out to the yard. Stephen tells me this is the only time we get to go outside, so I figure I'll go. What else is there to do?

9

For the first time I see prisoners from other wings. Some are mean looking, some are tough, and some are pretty regular. For some reason I again try to put on a "don't fuck with me" scowl, but a lot of these guys are the real deal and shit like that don't scare them.

Out in the yard I meet a guy from another cell. He's about my age and hyper. He's got a chatty, peppy personality and he's all smiles. He knows a few of the guys in there, and I get the impression he wants to know everyone the way he's striking up casual conversations. He talks to me in decent English. Jacque, his name is, and we pick up a football and start playing catch. The Montreal fan from the courthouse and van ride joins in too. Most of the guys out in the yard walk in circles, two or three of them together. Football gets boring and Stephen asks if I want to play catch with the softball and gloves. I haven't played catch in years! But it was great to throw around a bit.

I meet up with David from the van ride and he tells me there's a guy in D-wing from Arizona, another American. I figure it could do me some good to get to know him, so David calls him over. We talk about the good ol' U.S. of A. and play catch with the softball. He's a friendly guy, tells me he was supposed to be in for three to six months. Then his lawyer called and said one to two years. Last he'd heard, they were thinking three to five years. Tough break. His story gets me all kinds of nervous so I go take a seat with him and some of the guys from his wing. His guys are cool and calm. I like them exceedingly more than the dirty ones in my wing. The Arizona guy introduces himself as Mike and invites me to stay in D-wing instead of C.

"Yeah, you should come over to our side. We clean it every day, mop, sweep, wash the table. Everyone has their own job, it's great. Unlike that pigpen you stay in."

"Ha, you don't have to tell me how shitty that place is. Believe me, I know."

"Come to the gym tonight, they'll open it up about four o'clock, I'll hook you up, we'll get the guards to let you come into D-wing," he tells me.

David is sitting with us, and Mike turns and tells me, "You see this guy, they can't keep him locked up." To David, he asks, "Hey, how many times have you escaped?"

"Haha, three times in three months," David tells us, but he won't say how.

"You escaped three times, and they keep catchin' you and bringing you back? What the hell is wrong with you?" Mike asks.

"Well, what am I supposed to do man? I can't leave the country, I can't really travel."

"You're a freak, you know that. I'm gonna call you David Blane from now on!" says Mike.

Our hour outside is up, so we shuffle back into the dank zoo. Bear is back at his popsicle sticks, Speedy and Crackhead stayed in the cell, and Stephen and I sit back down at the table. I open the book and read for an hour until the gym opens up.

The gym has a ping-pong table, pool table, bench press, some dumbbells, and a leg press. It has one of those cable machine things too. Eager for some physical exercise, I jump on the stair stepper and warm up a bit. Mike comes in with a few fellas from his side.

"Hey kid how ya doin'? You wanna get a good shoulder work out in?"

"Ah, I can't do much with a barbell 'cause of my wrist. I gotta use dumbbells."

"Alright, well we'll be on the bench over there. These guys all saw me throw up 350 on the bench when I first got here, now nobody fucks with me. haha."

It felt good to exercise a bit, and I went about a pretty mild workout, back and biceps. Not Mike though, that guy doesn't mess around. Five minutes in I'm on my third set, and Mike's shirt is already soaked at the collar. He's throwing up obscene amounts of weight at the military press, shoulders bulging, eyes popping, the vein at his temple pulsing with the strain. He's a different man in the weight room, intense and pretty demonic looking. *Ok, make mental note,* I think to myself, *stay on this guy's good side.*

I finish up in a half hour, but Mike's still ripping hard. So I stroll on over to the ping-pong table to pass the boredom. I put one side vertical and start playing by myself, but after a few minutes, Bear comes and joins me. We put the side down and have a speechless match. We speak no words, only body language. It's smiles and shrugs, nods and claps. But pretty soon, gym time's over. On the way back upstairs I talk to Mike about moving to his wing tomorrow.

But for now it's back to that cigarette haze in C-wing and it's already dinner time. The inmates are lined up at the bar like feeding dogs, call it pavlovian, call it *conditioned*.

The meal is a regular Thanksgiving supper, processed turkey, mashed potatoes, peas, and a grey gravy. It's pretty good, actually, a nice change of pace!

With dinner done, I'm sitting at the table with my book. It's a great story, and I'm the closet to enthralled one could be in my situation. It's going on seven o'clock, and I'm counting down the hours 'til it's back to the bullpen for me. And here comes speedy minus that puffed up ghetto hoodie he typically sports, towel in hand. Hey…maybe crack heads do take showers! How's that for a revelation?! HA! Like I'm one to talk, I ain't even jumped in yet. Reason being: I don't have sandals and I'm not fond of foot herpes. Which reminds me…I gotta order some stuff from the canteen. I find Stephen to help translate the list of items. I desperately want a pad of paper and a pen, that's all. Oh, plus shower sandals. Stephen helps me out—u*n stylo et papier.* Oh, how I want to write so dearly! I've sat in a cage, wasting and withering,

during a time when my writing should be most prolific. Yes, a pen and paper
is all I need.

Speedy's walking outta the shower, towel wrapped around a sickly,
emaciated frame. That hoodie is deceiving; Speedy looks like he would
crumble under my wrestling tie-ups, my forearm club. I'd hit him with a blast
double that knocks the wind out of his gut, takes him off his feet and drops
him on his head, then throw the legs in and torture his poor body. And oh how
I long to wrestle! How I long to be back with the team, a band of brothers
who've endured the sufferings of sucking weight, the misery of the never
ending season with its grueling practices and we would stumble out after
conditioning, adorned with black eyes and broken noses like badges of
courage and we knew we were a pound over and that means no water tonight!
We were there together, and people are drawn closet when they've
experienced such hardships together, when they've had to rely on each other
to pull them through, to endure and persevere with tenacious intensity. That is
wrestling, the individuality of competition, and so reliant on the team. And
people say it's not a team sport, HAH! In fact there is no greater sport than the
oldest sport, the most basic form of athletic competition, the primitive battle
between two egos, two conditioned warriors indifferent to both the pain he
issues and the pain he receives because pain is irrelevant to their triumph. And
just putting your foot on that line is a victory on its own. But the true triumph
is the sportsmanship, the wrestler who keeps his chin high and shakes his
opponent's hand with grace and candor after a heart-ripping loss. Yes,
wrestling is a thorough test of character from the most primitive physical level
to the wisest mental level through and through. I always knew I was tough, but

wrestling taught me how tough, wrestling pushed me to my breaking limits. It's because of wrestling that I sit here today, a confident and courageous person. Anything the world throws at me, the miseries of life on the road or in the wild or behind bars, I've already beaten it. For me, there is no quit. I simply adapt and do. Seriously, if you ever have the chance to experience wrestling, do it, "KID YOU"LL MOVE MOUNTAINS!"

This sucks, but I know I'm gonna look back at the experience, grateful for it and a better person because of it. See, people encounter hardship and crumble beneath its choke. But the wise man will learn all he can from the experience. I came into the journey with a defined purpose: that I would become more understanding and insightful as a result of what I experienced. I left thinking that the only way I could be justly and logically philosophical is if I had experienced the broad spectrum of lives and people. I consider this blessed opportunity a chance to empathize with prisoners.

With these scrabbling streams of thought, I feel my eyelids getting heavy. Sleep would be so nice right now. Sleep, in a nice, comfortable bed with new sheets fresh out of the dryer. The most comfortable bed I've had in two weeks was that mat last night in the bullpen, and I couldn't even enjoy it with those fucking French scumbags keeping me up. But oh how nice a nap would be in a cozy bed with blankets. I'm nodding off, "bobbing for cock" as my Marine buddy likes to call it. The last thing I want to do is nod off in this sty. I'll get shanked or raped or…

I'm nineteen years old in a place I don't belong. My imagination is not my friend.

Bullpen call for me, Crackhead, and that dirty truck driver from last night. We head on down, grab the mats and pillows and walk in. Son of a bitch, you gotta be fucking kidding me. There are six more dudes in there already, and I don't like it. The six new guys are all talking to each other like douche bags, and I think to myself they might have been in the same street gang or something. They're already chummy like they've known each other for years. Crackhead meets up with his dope friend and they gossip like school girls. I lay my mat out and make my bed, making sure to get a prime location in a corner so I'm not surrounded by swine. The bullpen is so crowded now that the mats barely fit. One guy sleeps on a table, another has his nose right under the toilet bowl—and what's disturbing is he doesn't even seem to mind, as if these living conditions are better than his previous ones. What a circus! Bazooko territory.

I'm already under the covers, but of course, the cocksuckers keep talking, 'til two in the fucking a.m. I can only imagine what they're saying.

"Yo man remember when we stole candy from those kids? 'member when we ruffied those bitches and tripped old ladies and peed on puppies and cursed obscenities at kindergarteners and other stuff delinquents with poor morals like us do? Haha, yeah dude that was sweet!"

Also, the kind guards leave the light on for us again. Oh, joy.

<u>10</u>

I wake up to Frosted Flakes for breakfast. This is pleasing. I never used to like them that much, but now they are a delicacy and I'm just smitten. Norman struggles with the milk carton again, his gimped thumb watching uselessly. Crackhead searches tremulously for his smokes, finds them, and he and his boyfriend light two up. And I'm thinking of a childhood so jubilant, of a time past. I'm tired and I still ain't showered and now it's starting to bother me. My hair slicks up on end, my excuse for a beard grows thin in patches, but the bright side: I think my odor should be potent enough by now to deter any potential acquaintances. Haha, defense tactics 101! Then I remember these are French Canadians and French Canadians suck at life in every possible way, my odor just may attract them like bees to pollen.

And so begins the defeating trudge back to C-wing.

...but wait! Oh yes! Not today, today I'm moving to D-wing! I tell the guards, who are new ones today, that I had been in D-wing all along and that I had my stuff in there. They let me in either out of the goodness of their hearts, or because they're French Canadian blood sucking leeches with the intelligence level of your average carrot (not Mary though, she's a nice guard). My guess is the latter.

D-wing is an oasis amidst the bowels of Sorel. Compared to the pig farm next door, D-wing is the Ritz of prison life. I walk in and Mike and a few others are awake and sitting at the table. He puts his finger to his lips saying shhh. This side is so organized and cooperative that they have instituted a policy of "no noise before 10 a.m." No showers, no flushing toilets (which are loud as hell, by the way), no yelling, and keep the TV volume low. I could get used to this.

Mike explains to me that everyone has his own roll, sweeping, mopping, etc. "I got here about two months ago; I was amazed when I came in. Everyone was helping out, keeping the place clean. I said, 'gimme a broom or something,' I feel like a bum with nothin' to do.'"

A man of about fifty walks up to the sink, razor and towel in hand. He was obviously the type who combed his hair, but hadn't since he woke up, and it stuck awkwardly out to the side.

Mike leans to me and says, "That's the fag of the wing. But he gives the other guys cigarettes, so they don't beat his ass."

I nod, thinking how sad a culture I'm immersed in.

The Fag rinses his face and sloshes on thick shaving cream. "He's gonna shave for the next 15 minutes, watch," Mike tells me.

Sure thing, the guy is obsessive. 15 minutes later and he's still going strong. Any more and he'll be shaving bone. The guy spent 27 minutes shaving his face. 27 minutes. I'm glad I'm not the tax payer paying the water bill. If you live in Quebec, know this: your tax money is being disgustingly and irresponsibly wasted. That is, if you pay taxes, I don't know how your circus world works. Either way, someone's money is being foolishly poured down the drain (for several reasons, The Fag's shaving ritual is just a facetious example).

Ten o'clock rolls around and one of the guys from the wing, Max, starts mopping the floor. Max is cool. Probably 21 or 22, 6'1" and pretty strong looking. He wears those oversized ghetto t-shirts that hang down to mid thigh. It sways methodically as he slides the mop from side to side. His shirt says "loyal to the game" and has a roll of hundies (hundred dollar bills) on it. Haha, that's sweet...*I WANT THAT SHIRT!* I think to myself. He's got headphones in and he bounces to a silent beat as he mops. I don't like meeting new people, and I don't like new places, but so far everyone seems cool. I thought I had just been getting used to the guys over in C-wing. Bear, Stephen, Crackhead, Speedy, Shifty and his abuser; I wonder what those guys are up to. I picture the innocent smile on Bear's rough face as he molds his models; I picture the mellowed out Stephen watching his French TV. Shifty was such a character, like someone out of a book. The type of character that exists only in books or movies, but there he was, alive and real right in front of my eyes!

The next guy to meander out toward the table looks like a Tony. He's cool and easy, backwards red hat and a confident, relaxed walk. He's got a bushy mustache and he's probably in his forties, but he's got a young demeanor, like he's 25.

"Hey ya cocksucker! Who the fuck was snoring last night?" he says to Mike. I'm glad to hear he speaks English easily, and his obscenities would prove to be amusing.

Mike introduces the two of us and we make small talk for a bit. The usual "where you from?" "What you in for?" stuff. He asks if I have any drugs on me in a tone that says he's only half-kidding.

The seconds crawl and the minutes blur as my eyes feel dryer and dryer. I lay my forehead on my book and fall asleep at the table. I don't get much sleep in that hellhole. I had been weary of napping over in C-wing, not knowing what kind of shit they might pull (again, it was probably just my imagination giving me a rough time), so I never napped. It caught up with me, and I guess I didn't realize I had really passed out on the table there. Tony wakes me up calmly.

"Hey man, you wanna sleep, you can go lie down in the corner over there. That's what I used to do. Here come with me; we'll get you set up."

Wow, what hospitality! Tony grabs a blanket and lays it on the granite floor for me. He even gets me a pillow!

"See, you come to our side, we take care of ya, not like that pig pen next door. You want anything, just ask. We got soda, snacks, we'll smoke some joints. We're cool over here," Tony tells me. Again I'm thinking to myself, *did I hear right? Did he say "smoke some joints?"* which leaves me pondering how the eff they get drugs into this place. I lie down on the cold, hard floor and get the best sleep I've had in a while. You know that sleep you crave when you're at your desk in class and your teacher just drones and drones in monotone and don't you wish that you were home?

Two hours later I wake up groggy and it's time for lunch. We get back with our trays and Mike and Tony actually make sure I have a seat at the table. The table holds eight people, which means three or four are left to eat while standing. Surprisingly, they let me usurp the spot of a guy none of them like too much. I've kept to myself the entire time, just staying friendly and quiet, and so far it's working cuz I haven't been stomped out yet. I consider this a plus.

At lunch I meet the rest of the guys. A feeble old man, knotted at the joints, sits to my left, big Italian nose and a happy smile on his face. The guy cracks me up; I can't imagine what he's in here for. He's gotta weigh less than a hundred pounds. The word "decrepit" comes to mind. The Fag sits across the table, along with Tony, Max, and a new guy, Pat. He's about 25 and has a rough, pockmarked face, a combination of his chain smoking and the days of an awkward adolescence. To my right looks like a Frank. This Frank is pretty strong looking, not huge, but not small either. He carries around a bit of extra weight, and he has a calm, quite face about him. In the corner sits Malloy, aka El Presidente, aka The Garbage Disposal. He's a fat slob of a man, always grumpy, always eating. If there's anything on your tray you don't want, you sacrifice it to the Garbage Disposal. Our lunchtime desserts were, again, shitty. Nobody would eat them, except Malloy...who ate seven.

Lunch is done and Tony, Pat, Mike, and Frank sit down to play cards. Tony likes to swear in English, Pat and Frank don't understand any. "Ah fuck! You cocksuckers get all the good cards, this is bullshit!" I'm reading my book at the table; the Fag is sitting next to me and the old man, across from him. The fag pulls out his tobacco and rolls one up quite deftly in his delicate hands, then passes it to the old man who puffs at it with gumby cheeks. Then the Fag rolls up another and offers it to me. I refuse but thank him, and he initiates some conversation. His English is poor and hard to understand, and the conversation is quickly over. Mike leans over and says in a voice not so hushed, "What's the fag want from you?" sarcastically.

I see the Fag look down and away meekly and I get the impression he understood the jeer. I also get the impression that he's used to it. I have yet to discover if he is, indeed, homosexual. In this primitive world it could just be a vicious rumor running slanderously wild—eighth grade reincarnated.

The day passes uneventfully. Dinner comes and goes (Malloy ate six pieces of cake) and I sit down to read and write. Mike tells me he's got the guys watching *Two and a Half Men* in English. "See, over here you at least get to watch some English TV." The news of *Two and a Half Men* makes me yearn for home again. I never liked the show, but I remember staying up to watch it with my mom back home. And now the notion of the show makes my heart wrench and roll. It is a hint of that beautiful and innocent past when I would stay up watching the mediocre show just to spend the time with my mother, who would work oh so hard and harder than any woman of her brilliance should have to and there we sat, not laughing but enjoying it and not so much the show but more each other's company and now I want to be back on the worn couch with its exhausted pillows that fold comfortably behind the crook of your neck (but all I have is this metal god damn bench) and I remember how we just sat there in silence because words were useless, because words would have only spoiled the moment, the mother-son bond and its tangible presence. I think of how ashamed and disappointed she would be to see where I am now and how I love her so much that I'm starting to hate myself for putting her through this inevitable choke of disappointment and oh why? god why?! I'm a college dropout, I'm in prison, I'm a regular scumbag. I picture the crushed look on her face when she would find out, standing heartbroken and shaken and assuming all responsibility for my failure. The emotion is there and I'm choking up now; Mike mentions the show and it brings a warm nostalgia that quickly turns sour and puckers my jaw tense. I'm swallowing hard and fending off tears because this is not the place for it! So I think of what I could say to explain myself, to justify what I've done. The justification is there, but most people stop at the surface. College Dropout. Convict. Homeless. The labels I'll be plagued by because people are too superficial to consider explanation, too concerned with digging up the next slanderous gossip so they can talk about everyone else's faults to avoid their own. These are people beneath reason, insight, or wisdom. These are people who live such empty lives that they fill their hollow soul with reassuring and fallacious labels that tell them they're just super. These are the kind of people who read only headlines; they're prejudicial, conniving leeches who suck the glory out of deserving people so they don't have to face the pathetic void they dwell in. These are the real scumbags.

But I did nothing unethical. I did nothing I'm ashamed of, nor should I be. I contribute and try to bring happiness to people. I want to spread knowledge, laughter, and truth. What is the purpose of a prison? A prison corrals all the wrongdoers, the burdens of society, the scum who take and never give, and locks them up behind bars, never to bother contributing good-samaritans. A prison removes these animals from the streets (the crack heads, murderers, rapists, and thieves that I'm surrounded by) because they are deemed unfit for society. And by such logic, I do not belong. I DO NOT BELONG! But unfortunately law and justice are not synonymous. And so, I dare proclaim that I am not the criminal. Rather, those who sit and waste a blessed life, those who fail to realize their potential, the ones afraid to *do*, those are the true criminals. The atrocity of our era is the mind that dare not question—and their heads will nod to the brainwash beat, the song that confuses the masses into a chaotic conundrum where they're fooled into thinking their precious little lives are worth while. And perhaps worse is the criminal who uses the pathetic majority as what they are rather than spreading truth and exposing the deeper beauties of life. I think of Hitler and Stalin, I think of the fallacies of democracy (the ignorant majority). I think of how my stories are seen as controversial and I wonder *why?* I know why, and it's because I know why that I don't care. You know, if people weren't so fucking uptight or worried about how they're seen by other people, we'd have a lot fewer problems. But people will always be insecure, people will always look to exploit your faults and don't think for a second that it's because they're better than you. Have confidence in what you do and why you're doing it. Listen, we're all a bit fucked up, but the really fucked up ones are the people who pretend with that pretentious "I'm better than you" bullshit façade. I'm just sick of people being ashamed for the things we all do; I'm sick of lies perverting truth. And isn't that partly why I left in the first place? Tired of the futile bickering between people, I just wanted to get away, to subjugate myself to solitude and find serenity—time well spent with the silent soul in desolation is oh so humbling, a needed diversion from the path of the banal menagerie of people and their ordinary, boring lives. Oh sigh, it's not for me.

We watch the show and let time play, and after the show Mike tells me I can wash my clothes. He gets a bucket and I fill it with hot water. He gets the soap and I pour some in. Longing a shower now, I ask him how to buy sandals, but the guy's so great. He brings some out for me saying, "Here, use these." I throw my worn, dirty clothes in the bucket to soak and grab my towel for the long awaited shower. The water isn't just warm like I had expected, it's *hot!* The hot water runs down my body, the shower head tickles my back with its spray and it just feels so *good!* When I get out, Pat has one of his t-shirts and a pair of basketball pants for me. Damn, talk about hospitality. It's amazing what a hot shower will do to boost morale. I feel like a new man, I can actually crack a smile now as I sit at the table with the other guys.

And pretty soon it's time to head on down to the bullpen, so much for the smile. Mike tells me he'll take care of my clothes and lay them out to dry when they're done soaking, so I'm on my way down stairs. yay.

Back in the bullpen there are some new guys. There is a kid about my age, shaved head and big teeth that give him a cartoonish appearance, an old fat French fuck with a mustache and unhealthy looking body, a guy who must be in his forties, but acts like he's twelve, a creepy looking dude who I thought looked like an Amish gangsta, and a black guy with a terrorist-looking beard. He's only the second black guy I've seen at this place, he's sitting on the table talking to a few of the others. I set my paper pad (in which I've written about twelve pages thus far) down on the bench and start to make my mat. At this point I'm pissed 'cause I don't like the look of any of them, and I can tell they too are gonna stay up all fucking night talking. When I look up to grab my pillow, I notice the black guy has his foot on my pad of paper and it's ripped up some now. This inferiorities me, as he is fucking with my writing and my writing is all I got in this place. I've poured heart and soul into that pad and his blatant disregard for my things snaps a gasket.

"What the FUCK, ASSHOLE!" I shout. (Yes, I know he might be in some gang with those other guys. Yes, I know I might get a beating. Yes, I know cursing disrespectful obscenities is grounds for such things, but at this point I really just don't care. I'm beyond worrying about physical abuse, what more are they gonna do? By this point, physical beatings are nothing because I am all mind. In times of such hardship, you'll hit a threshold point where you'll realize that the mind is so much stronger and; thus, capable of both shutting out physical pain and causing astronomically worse (mental) pain. As long as I stay tough mentally, there is nothing he or they can do. Pussies.)

He looks at me like he has no idea why I said that, so I point at my paper pad. To my surprise he apologizes, he even looks scared like he was the one who might get a beat down.

As I could have guessed, these French rats stayed up late talking stupid. This batch of grime even managed to make this night the most miserable one so far. The "40 year-old who acted like he was 12" was despicable. Every two minutes he would rip ass and laugh like he was in grade school at the cafeteria, and all the other bastards would chime in too. Guys, it's not that fucking funny after a couple dozen times, *merry freaking Christmas!* I listened to them slur their drunken French slang and butcher what people once called "the most romantic language." Most romantic, huh? Spend a night in the bullpen and tell me that! They were loud and crude, they were savages. The "40 year-old who acted like he was 12" even dropped trou and took a shit in the disease infested toilet…you make me sick. Four hours of hoots and grunts and slurring *"je pas e"* shit later I fell asleep to sweet dreams of me cutting their fucking throats and watching their useless life leak from their broken veins. Yeah, I'm fucked up. Old news.

11

In the morning we get All-Bran cereal…it is shitty. Then it's back up to D-wing.

The black guy with the beard also gets put into D-wing, so does Norman today for some reason. I can't say I'm pleased to see Norman back, but what are ya gonna do?

Mike tells the new guys the 10 a.m. rule and we sit down at the table to catch up on some good ol' French TV. I'm pretty into my book now, and when I'm not reading, I write some—little observations here and there, streams of conscious thought, that sorta thing. At 10 a.m. I grab a broom and start sweeping so Max can mop. Once the floor is cleaned up a bit, Norman heads down to the corner to pass out, and I decide to do the same.

An hour later I'm hovering in that dream-awake stage and I kind of hear the guys from the wing getting loud. They had been playing cards, so I was used to the nonchalant *"fuckin' cocksuckers"* type stuff, but something about this sounded hostile. I open my eyes to see Max and Pat pushing Mike at the shoulders as if to hold him back. Mike's red in the face, looking the same sort of intense that he does in the weight room. He's wearing a wife-beater shirt that reveals pumped arms with tribal tattoos running up and down them like vines. He's fuming about something and I don't know what...red flag—I better be on my toes.

I sit up and hear Mike yell, "What's that fucker's name? Norman? I'LL FUCKING BREAK HIS NECK!"

I better move.

As I get up I see Mike pick up something metal and whip it at the sleeping Norman, but the other guys manage to keep the bull held back.

Tony is talking sense into Mike saying, "Hey, man the game's on tonight, I don't wanna get put in lockdown. Come on man, I wanna watch the game. We'll do it tomorrow."

This calms Mike and they negotiate to issue Norman's beating tomorrow—unbelievable, it's like a business transaction.

So I waltz over to the table and sit next to the now simmering Mike. "Hey kid, sorry I woke ya," he says to me.

"Oh, it's fine, I was getting up anyway. So what's up?" I ask.

"Well apparently that guy Norman transferred into D-wing 'cause the guys in his old wing were gonna beat his ass. Turns out, Norman's in for raping a 13 year-old girl. The guy's 31!" He then proceeded to explain the finer points of prison etiquette to me. "See, even criminals look down on some people. In prison, three types of people aren't well liked: Pedophiles, snitches, and rapists. If you're a rapist or a snitch and you get thrown in jail, you get your ass beat. The guys in the other wing found out about Norman and were about to beat him so he moved in here, like we wouldn't find out."

Now, I'm sitting here bewildered. I remember Norman telling me he was in for "trafficking…long time." Turns out, the scum bag is a rapist. Good, let him get the shit kicked outta him.

"Last month I was in here," Mike continues, "and there was a young kid in, 22 or something, nice kid. I was talking to him, laughing and joking, and suddenly he just snapped. A new guy came into our wing, he was in his cell. The kid walked over to the cell, walked in and locked the cell door. He just started unloading on the guy, so unexpected—just hammering fists and elbows on the guy. Well we had to get the guards to open the door up and break them up, but the kid had pretty much beaten the dude unconscious—bloody mess. Turns out, that guy had snitched on the kid's brother and got him thrown in jail. Guys don't mess around here."

"So, Norman's gonna get his beating tomorrow?" I ask.

"Yeah, you want a story, kid? Come out to the yard tomorrow, I'll give you a story."

So here I'm sitting and thinking, *shit, this is real life behind bars—beatings at the yard and all.* The Montreal game was going to be on tonight, so the guys decided to do the beating tomorrow. See, if you get rambunctious, the guards put all the prisoners in lock down, which means no TV to see the game. It was so strange to me, this beating *needed* to happen for these guys, as though it was inevitable. So after that, Saturday passed by pretty uneventfully. I read, I wrote. I watched the Fag roll tobacco joints for himself and the old man. I watched the two of them smoke fiendishly. Malloy swallowed obscene quantities of desserts and soda, Tony was cool, Max bounced to his headphones, and Norman sat in the far corner, anxiously awaiting the inevitable abuse that was sure to come soon. We watch Montreal lose the hockey game in a close match, which means riots in the streets. After that...bullpen time.

The bullpen was the same repulsive group of guys. More flatulence jokes, more drunken slur, less sleep. I was hoping none of them understood or spoke English, the last thing I wanted to do was strike up a friendly conversation of frolicking times past with one of these repugnant slugs. But of course, the fat slob with his bushy mustache and greasy face starts talking nice with me like we were old time pals. This does not brighten my day, but I carry on a conversation, I was even mildly nice to him. Then he ripped ass and bellowed his ugly French laugh. I rolled over and closed my eyes pretending to sleep.

<u>12</u>

We woke up and grabbed our breakfast trays, a few of the guys started smoking, and the fat slob asked for my coffee so I threw the piping hot drink right into his eyes. Haha, no I was kidding, but that would have been sweet, right?

Back in D-wing Norman waits timidly in his corner. Mike and most of the other guys are still asleep, so I take a seat and start to read again. In an hour or so, I'm done with the book and bored, looking for anything to do. The day is a slow one, and through the barred windows I see it's overcast. It's been raining lightly on and off and grey skies look sad and dreary. Well, the poor weather keeps us from being able to go out to the yard, so we're stuck in doors, which raises the question: where will Norman get his beating? I would soon find out.

Instead of going outside, they let us in the gym, but not many go. I do a chest and triceps workout and go play ping-pong while Frank and Mike pump iron like gladiators ready for battle. They're throwing around barbells as heavy as NFL linebackers with a vengeance.

We get back to D-wing and for some reason Mike miraculously grows a soft spot for Norman. Mike tells him he's going to be getting the beating soon, and Norman kind of shrugs and smiles nervously. Tony, Frank, and Pat are caballing in the corner, devising their plan to jump Norman. Mike does Norman the courtesy of telling him that he had better get his ass out of D-wing and quick, 'cause the beating is on its way. Suddenly Norman realizes that Mike ain't fuckin' around. He waltzes his lanky, bird-like body over to the door, his stupid hair bobbing on his crack-aged face. At this moment I'm writing at the table, sitting next to the decrepit old man. *I watch him wait, frightened and anxious, for the beating to come—the inevitable beating. He knows it's coming, we all know it's coming, but when? And so he deteriorates, not knowing when and always waiting, wondering. It is a well known fact that the human mind will nearly consume itself in waiting for such things. The imagination can be far worse than the actual event. And now he hangs his head, twiddles his good thumb around that dead thumb on his right hand, head hung in defeat.*

At the door, Norman pukes his rotten French, calling for the guards to move him to the protective wing. As he turns around to collect his stuff, he walks into the wall of Tony, Frank, and Pat. Before he even has time to throw his hands up, Frank is dropping a hammer of a fist with his thick arms down on Norman's face. The first slug drops him with that eerie sound of fist on flesh. Once down, Tony steps in with kicks to the ribs and Pat is at his head, sending punch after furious punch down at Norman's breaking face with such ferocity. I watch his skinny skull bounce off the tile like a basketball and the dull sound (so hollow, oh so hollow!) is starting to make me feel sick. My adrenaline is pumping now as I watch this helpless human being having his body pulverized. The blood is running through the cracks of the tiles now, dripping hauntingly down the drain (I think of horror movies, serial killers and their victims' blood). I know the guy deserves it, but still, I can't help but feel badly watching this. I close my eyes, not wanting to see more, but I squint one open because I have to see more. My open eye catches a glint of Norman's nose, broken and cracked diagonally. His eye is hidden under a mess of blood and his swollen face. His neck bends awkwardly under the force every time it bounces off the tile. His hands aren't even up; I think he's lost consciousness. It is as if sound has halted all together, everything seems slow motion, screams and yelps are muffled by the thunderous booming of fists on face, head on tile, swinging foot thudding in rib cage. The guards are rushing in, clubs raised, breaking up the torture, ripping the bodies thrashing fists trying to get one last blow in. Norman is wheeled out in critical condition and we're rounded up like cattle and huddled into the cages for our insolence. In the cage I have a lot of time to think, and all that haunts my mind is the violence I had just witnessed. I rationalize it; justify what it was that I was seeing. The man raped a thirteen year old girl, worthless, pitiful piece of shit. You ruin a girl's life at thirteen and get off with a beating?...Fuck you, scumbag, you get off easy.

13

The next day everyone is quiet. Mike wants the story recapped to him, he was in the shower at the time of the beating, and he's outraged that they didn't wait for him. Tony reassures him, "We got him, don't worry, we got the fucker."

"I told you to wait 'til I got outta the shower!" Mike protests.

Tony's feeling strung out and asking all around if anyone knows where he can get some drugs. He's about to go on a rampage. Apparently some guy just got back from the hospital and he's back in one of the cells. He had promised Tony that he would bring back some drugs with him, saying he could get seven grams of weed and all. Well, I guess he didn't fulfill his promise, and in prison, your word is all you're worth, so this guy's worth shit. The guy pokes his head out of his cell. He's got long wavy hair that sits stylishly on his head, not a bad looking guy. He's wearing glasses that give him the look of a scholar, or a philosophy professor. The Scholar did manage to bring back a dime or so; though, and it went straight to Tony. But Tony is a generous guy, and he's not above sharing.

It's a long, boring Monday, painfully boring. Mike tells me about the classes they offer. *Matematiques* and *Frances*. But he tells me the math ain't no multi-variable calculus, it's fractions and multiplication. "Seriously, these guys come in off the streets. They don't know simple math so that's all they offer here. I mean, these guys are street smart, but as far as schooling goes, they just don't know much. I mean, I'm not a genius, but I walked in goin' 'what the hell is this?'" But at this point, even mindless 5 * 5 busy work would be better than the grueling nothingness. Just before dinner, Tony's shaping a can, which can only mean one thing—they're blazin' soon. They make a pipe out of the can and head into his cell. He lights it up and pretty damn quickly, the hall reeks of marijuana. Way to be inconspicuous, bud. He passes it around to a few of the guys, but I don't jump in. I don't wanna get caught; I should be getting out real soon. I would have loved to live this world with Mary Jane, see the inner beauty, the anthropological thought would stream so prolifically, my mind would pour in beauty and psychological analysis. But I'm managing just fine without her, and I'm gonna keep it that way.

But I'm still wondering how the hell they get the stuff in here. I ask Mike. When I do, he looks at me with this mischievous smirk, doesn't say any words, just lightly taps me on the ass. "Now you know."

....yeah, I was speechless too. It took me a minute to let this absorb. Apparently dealing in prison is quite lucrative. You can sell for 400% higher than you can on the street. Guys slip a couple rocks or a few grams of this or that up their asshole, wrapped in bags. Yes. I know.

And that's the other reason I wasn't keen on smoking.

So now it's time for dinner and the guys who just smoked have a nice case of the munchies. They're shoveling down the best tasting food they've had in ages like primates, not even using utensils. They put Malloy to shame!

After dinner, they're giddy like school girls! Giggling and playing grab ass and triumphantly jubilant! It's a great sight to see grown men, convicts and criminals, dancing around and joking loud and innocently. What is this, summer fun camp for them?! Good for them, I wish I could dance right now.

I leave the high and stoned to head down to the bullpen. Just me and the black guy (who turned out to be nice, from Haiti, in for armed robbery (also, I'd like to add, I hate when people generalize the term "African American" to encompass all black persons. People think they're being so high and mighty when they use this "politically correct" term. It's not "politically correct," not all black people are of African descent, and they might not even be American. The assertion is both presumptuous and ignorant. Glad that's out of the way.) Back at the bullpen it's the same old story. Crack heads suck at their tobacco sticks, vile French creatures fart and snore their way through the night, and I, surprisingly, get a good night's sleep. I guess I've assimilated to the shitty conditions. It seems that the trend of my dreams has leaned toward women, beautiful women, during my stay at Sorel. I vaguely remember bits and pieces of my dreams the mornings after and their always involving some girl I've liked back home. Well, tonight's dream was vivid:

She's back in my life, my first girl, that aching disease. She's what I want her to be. It's late at night and the air sings and we are drunk or stoned or both. She lies next to me 'neath cool sheets, her warm skin against mine. My hand runs down her smooth waist line, the delicate slope of her angelic body, and she turns her head to kiss my lips. Our lips touch slow and sensual and I taste her sweet soft tongue. Propped up on my elbow, I brush her hair back, exposing her neck. She looks away, vulnerable and trusting, and I slide my kisses down the supple slope of her neck. She melts against my body as I slide my hand up the inside of her thigh. She rolls to face me and I climb on top of her, she traps me in her open thighs and hugs my body close. Warm chest on soft breasts, our thighs intertwined, we lie pelvis to pelvis and I slide inside her warm and wet. I stare into her beautiful trusting eyes, then lean in for another kiss but now the passion begins to boil. It's more tongue than lips, her breath is hot and slow and I'm riding in her like a wave caressing a shy shore under the moonlit midnight. The moonlight watches from the open blinds, casting a blue, mellow hue on the night scene. An ironically lonely hue because here we are, me with her and her with me and we are one together, passion and love and *lust!* And now I'm pulsing in her harder and deeper, pushing my body off of hers with straight arms braced on the bed, my chest is red and flexed and strong. She crawls her hands up my sides and braces them on my chest as if to feel my heart beat in synch with hers and so I lay my head down at her breast to do the same. I slow my rhythm and pull out to lay kisses in a row from her neck, through her breasts, and down that shapely stomach, oh she's so incredible. I hook her strong, lean thighs and she rolls on top, straddling me, her hands braced on my pumping chest. The sheet slips off one shoulder exposing that feminine clavicle, shadowed sexy by the moonlight. She finds me and sits on me and begins to rock so sensually, eyes closed, back arched, head thrown back—she's lost in some serenity. I grab her sloping waistline, oh the way the moonbeam makes those teasing shadows on her strong athletic core and I nearly shoot up right there. She's riding me hard now, posting my trotting hips with effortless rhythm. We're meant to be together, we're moving like one, breathing in harmony, and sexing to the sweet canorous song of each other's souls. She's humping me hard now, pure sex and sweat, her thighs slapping mine and now I grab her at the waist and shove her over so I'm on top and thrusting into her like passion's muscle, she whimpers virginally, pure pleasure, pure erotic pleasure. Her breathing is fast and deep and hot and wet against my neck and I can feel my pelvis sliding on top of her pubic bone, so I pull up and work her clitoris. As I wrap my arms around her steaming body and kiss my cheek to hers I feel me coming. I push inside her strong and driving and I shoot up deep inside her. With every rope she gasps a moan, her nails digging into my back like claws, and when I'm empty she releases with a sigh of satisfaction. And it's more kissing, more love, such *strong* and *true* love that I look through her deep dark eyes and see her soul and my reflection and I know she's happy for life because I'm with her and she's with me. And that's my girl, my aching disease—if only dreams came true—

14

I wake up with an erection, thinking of a way to grab my tray without the world knowing. I ask the black guy to grab mine; he does and it gives me just enough time to relax. I eat my breakfast sans Norman and his thumb. He's either in the hospital, or sore and aching in the protective wing. Poor Norman with his dumb, idiot hair, caked in blood; poor Norman and his disfigured face, no longer sickly and skinny looking. I hate myself for feeling sorry for him. I think if more people could witness atrocities, truly watch them with their own eyes, they would have a much more empathetic understanding of their effects. I watched this beating, I almost wish I could have experienced the raping, maybe then my sympathy for the crack head, scumbag Norman would be extinguished.

But that's the problem with people and their opinions, that's the problem with a lot of politics. Grossly rich politicians who live in a completely different world than the one we know are the people making the decisions. And they'll pretend to understand us; they'll pretend to empathize with our hardships, but they're just sly-lying their way to the top. It's a game with them and they'll say anything to level up. Part of my motivation on these "adventures" is that I want to live it all. I want to experience, first hand, poverty, middle class, and LA superstardom. I want to experience life in the wild, life on the road, and life in the joint; and then from there I'll deduce my thoughts and philosophies. I'm sick of listening to rich politicians, so far removed from the lifestyles of the people they influence, preach about how the tax payers' money should be spent. "What do you know?" I feel like asking them, "you've got tons of it." I want to live the life of a hardworking man, proud of every penny he earns. I want to live the life of a homeless wanderer just trying to survive on the basic needs. But we have to sit back and vote between "a giant douche" and a "turd sandwich" (thank you, Southpark, for the delicious symbolism), watch them pretend to be our friends with their plastered, manufactured smiles, their forced and deliberate speeches, they'll say anything for our vote.

Now, I'm not saying politicians are bad people, and I'm not about to start whining and preaching like I know politics (though, in an idealistic utopia, anarchy is the only way to live) because I, too, am parochial in my worldly views. But I think of the politicians on the news right now, and I think, how can they possibly relate to us? They can't because they're so far removed from the world *we* live in. I think of Chris, how he once told me that he doesn't like the idea of "politician" being a career. One shouldn't run for office because s/he is a "politician;" rather, one should run because s/he thinks s/he can offer the citizens a better quality life, or because s/he has developed a sophisticated sense of how the citizens could best be guided. It shouldn't be about parties or "conservative vs. liberal" because those are labels, and once we've labeled ourselves, we often feel obligated to always adhere to that parties latest ideas/beliefs/implementations. And so we see America split 50/50 (ish) between Democrat and Republican. Well, I bet we could have a modern day Hitler run under one party and people would be so jaded by their party's label that the ratio would still be far too close to 50/50 for comfort. It's a twisted world we live in, and in this world, you're either this or that or well on your way to becoming one or the other. No, I'm not one to trust the majority.

The majority is the perpetrator of the cyclic demise of man's individuality. So ensues the surrender of free will. So ensues the suppression of natural curiosity, the perversion of justice, and the stagnation [StagNATION] of progress. Above us cackles the voice of the structure at its triumph over the whole—a narcissistic puppet master that stares down from black onto the playground of happy children. We want our recess; we want our innocence, ACKNOWLEDGE OUR INDIVIDUAL SOVERIGNTY. But we're bred as machines from the start, and for it, the persistence of greed, hunger, and power will never be extinguished. To many, life is but a single-staircase, a mindless succession from one step to the next. Go to school, get a degree, mold your personality to the image we tell you to!

The American college student is
a dry-heaving parasite—
shrouded, coughing, a knife in the
rib of contribution.

119

He does not sing.
He wails and shouts
and pukes at Sunday Morning Mass.
His aim is a degree. His aim is nothing.
The educational system is
decadent depraved delusional.
Mail order diplomas, stick a 42 ¢ stamp on 'em
and send it across America.
Packaged credentials are a golden ticket to the
corporate ladder.
Life plateaus.

Why is it necessary to be stacked like slabs of meat, ranked and
flanked like cattle? Because standardization is the starting point for the
cleansing process. Back to the old drawing board, wipe it clean and start from
scratch! *Tabala Rosa!!* **and my knees will bounce to the brainwash
beat.**

And the puppets danced
On the jewelry box
While the world went around—

—Deceit, delusion, destruction, devolution, BEASTS! Things fall
apart. We are all such primitive monsters, so impressionable. Have we
forgotten our individual sovereignty? Have we become so processed by ritual
that any talk of anarchical angst will immediately be declared blasphemous?
So be it.

Laughter lied and love died.
God ejaculated cancer.
Irony's eyes smiled and cried.
The lonely found the answer—

120

Back at D-wing, Max is moving his stuff out.

"Is he gettin' out?" I ask Mike.

"Nah, not yet, he's just moving to another wing. Hey, let's get the guards to give you his cell!" Getting his cell would be a blessing. I'm ten days into my sentence, and I'll be leaving in just a few more days, but his cell would mean no more bullpen, no more sleeping on the cold granite floor, no more having to read and write in the loud lounge.

Some of the other guys are eager for haircuts. They've talked the guards into letting them use some clippers and they're starting to give each other buzz cuts. Mike leans over to me and says, "I think I'd trust the Fag more to cut my hair, hahaha! Oh, and by the way, kid...I read your diary thing, sorry. I got bored."

"Eh, I don't mind, I was planning on making it a book anyway," I told him, though I was a bit annoyed he had read it. Thankfully I hadn't really said anything too bad in it.

"Well, the guy really is gay," (I had written, *I have yet to find out if the Fag is, in fact, homosexual.*) "We caught him makin' out with another guy in one of the cells a couple weeks ago."

I'm still skeptical, but it really doesn't matter. Pat and the Fag take turns buzzing some of the guys. They're cracking jokes in French, and it's an all around relaxed morning, high spirits and prison friendships. The TV is on some French music video channel, mostly they all suck, until...CALABRIA! That bumpin' song by Enur starts playing and I'm reminiscent of days back at the RIT when I'd be high or happy with my entourage. I'd play this song and we start dancin' like nightclub chicks, hips-a-twistin' and feet-a-bouncin' (maybe that was just me) like we had no cares in the world, nothing to be embarrassed about but a reluctance to dance like life's too quick (which was never the case, cause we danced like we were dying tomorrow and that's how we used to live). Life was one joke after another, and in our down time we were laughing.

So now this *fabulousss* song's playing on the TV, and would you believe the scene that followed?!

Grown men, criminals, convicts, and inmates, start dancing like it's another drunken jubilance kinda night on the outside. Here are these prisoners pop lock n' droppin' with big ol' smiles smeared ear to ear on their faces. The delicious beat creeps into my ears and down my spine and next thing I know, my shoulders are boppin' in rhythm, then my arms. My knees are getting curious and I just can't suppress the urge to dance! I jump up on the table in my most loquacious act thus far and start workin' my hips like a night time female stripper at the gentlemen's club. My hips are rollin' and I'm booty droppin' like I got illegitimate kids to feed and now my hands are pulling my shirt up teasingly. I think the only thing hotter than the video was the room full of prisoners pseudo-stripping and dancing together.

After that, morale is high high high and I feel myself finally start to loosen up. I laugh loud and hearty and throw some jokes out of my own. I even crack some funnies at El Presidente, Malloy (who has finished off 48 cans of Pepsi and two quarts of grape sugar drink in 3 days, the guy's invincible or something).

After Max moves out, the guy's tell me I'll be getting his cell. This is pleasing news.

I lay my sheets out and make my bed, my nice cozy bed. Now I have a cell to myself, my own toilet, my own bed! I can go to bed early, I can actually get some sleep, and I can write in peace! Around nine o'clock I go into my new cell to write and rest.

I want to write a poem, but the words and thoughts just aren't coming to me. I want to say something equivocal about these faded yellow walls, the cracking paint. I think about the blue-grey bars (more grey than blue) and I want to say something about how dreary they look, how this whole place is overcast weather. The dull yellow walls, like the glow of a tired sun creeping through grey clouds, or the way the bars make lonely shadows on the walls—I want this poem in writing. But now I realize, maybe this isn't a poem, maybe this is something greater. I'm living this fantasy, stop writing and finish living it first! Life isn't one poem after another; poems are what we do when life isn't happening. I think back to Stephen, the attempted murderer. I think back to his story of heroin and whiskey and stabbing and murder and rage, and my dumb ass saying, "It'd make a good poem." His response, so priceless. "Pshh, a poem? Shit." That humbling response that snapped me out of the dream land I was arrogantly floating in was so needed, and so timely. Such brilliance from a source so unexpected, but I was there and dared to question—you never know where such treasures are hidden. This isn't a poem; this is a fucking story, and an amazing story at that! And it ain't over, I'm still living it. I put my pad and pen down and sit back against the wall, truly resting for the first time and absorbing this story.

I fall asleep for the first time without the bath of cigarette smoke and without the repulsive lullaby of those French bastards flatulating and snoring through black cancered lungs—life is swell with no more bullpen.

15

The next morning I can sleep in a bit longer without the guards crashing their sticks on the bars—the perks of having a cell. Today should be my last full day, tomorrow I'll be headed back to court, then hopefully on my way back to the beautiful USA and I think of baseball and apple pie, hot dogs and summer sun dresses, blue skies and sidewalk chalk—the land of the free and home of the brave, the epitome of my finale and the summation of this unholy journey.

And so begins the agonizing boredom. But the new cell means I can at least nap to pass the time. I go in and lie down, set my pad and pen on the shelf, and start to doze off.

It's about 10 a.m. when I hear the guard call for me in his dumb sounding accent. I roll out of bed and meet him at the door. He takes me down stairs and back into the bullpen where Speedy, Crackhead, and a few other inmates are pacing around, one is the kid about my age with the shaved head and big teeth, and, as if I weren't pissed off enough already, the 40 year old who acts like he's 12 is also there (what is this, a surprise party? who invited all my friends!). Speedy sees me and stops mid step, opens his arms wide and triumphant-like, saying, "Heyy, AmeriKan! hahaha!" I can't help but crack a smile when I hear the familiar optimism in his raspy yell. I ask him why they have us here, what's going on, and he tells me it's because we're going to court. But my court date isn't until tomorrow...*could I be getting out a day early? And if so, how am I gonna get my stuff back? I gotta give Pat his clothes back, I left my writings in my cell, I gotta say goodbye to Mike!*

I ask the guard if I can go back, but the son of a bitch is curt and short with me, and doesn't understand my English. Well, it's no problem; I'll just get the stuff after court. We're searched and cuffed individually, then marched out of the bullpen, back through the bowels of the prison, and into the garage where that van waits to take us into the courthouse in St. Jean.

We shuffle into the van and all the guys immediately pull out three rolled cigarettes and start passing them around, so begins my menthol shower. Speedy entertains us with his wild antics, his banging on the cage and swearing at the guards, *"tar ba nock!"* Crackhead booms his wheezy laughter though a wide open mouth, exposing those rotten, dying teeth. I'm lucky enough to be sitting right next to him, and his stench is near unbearable—a combination of French body odor (spoiled cheese and vinegar wine) and old cigarette ash, which cakes his gums black like tar. I stick my elbow out at an awkward angle so it jabs him in his ribs anytime he wanders too near. Every time I spear him, he squirms like an injured rodent and slides his putrid body over, and I have to suppress a mildly sadistic smile of gratification. They're all obnoxious and loud, but we're almost an hour into the ride and I know it won't be much longer 'til we're there. They've smoked through their tobacco fix, and Crackhead is back to his itching-twitching. His eyes get wide and he grins a rotten smile as he spots a cigarette butt on the floor of the van, giving him an uncanny resemblance to Smeagle from the *Lord of the Rings* movies. I can almost hear him rasping, *"preciousss!"* as he dives to the floor in pitiful desperation. He's lying at our feet, crawling his cuffed hands under one of the benches for the cigarette butt that's just out of reach, but his incorrigible will pays off, and he manages to pinch the filter end between dirty, stubby paws, fingernails yellow and caked black around the edges (ugh, and to think, these guys share those cigarettes). Crackhead, ecstatic with his glorious triumph, quickly shoves the butt (which has clearly been stepped on and sitting in the dankness of the van and who knows whose lips it's touched before) into his raw lips and Speedy helps him light up. There is literally a quarter inch of tobacco left in the thing, Speedy is actually lighting mostly filter. This should give you an accurate idea of how sickly desperate these wastes are. Crackhead draws in the burning filter (like it matters to him, he's no doubt smoked worse) and hands the butt over to Speedy. As Speedy sticks it in his lips, the quiet guy in the corner says something in French (This guy is wearing some peculiar garb, rubber boots and a jump suit type thing. He's been quiet the entire ride, taking puffs of the cigarettes in turn, and other than that he's kept to himself. I remember how he sat taciturn and expressionless, but always looking pensive. I thought to myself that he was the truly dangerous type; smart and demented, that serial-killer vibe. I later found out his name was

Jean). Well, Jean says something in French, not hostile or threatening-sounding in anyway, something that sounds like *"poco."* I know *"poco"* in Spanish is "small" or "little" but I don't know if that's anything related to what Jean said. Jean's comment sets Speedy off on a slurring French tirade. He starts swearing and hissing threats at Jean (and I so much wish I could understand, but body language is all I'm spared). He throws the cigarette butt at Jean, and it sparks all over him and the man next to him. But Speedy keeps the insults flying. He yells something at Jean and motions to the floor, and then repeats it. Suddenly Jean hobbles to his knees and bows his head, whispers something, and looks up into the twisted eyes of his dominant. Speedy smirks with cocky gratification, and the guy at my right leans over to bump fists, hands still in cuffs. Jean sits back up in his seat, defeated and ashamed and wishing he weren't here right now. And that's how prison works, it is a hierarchy based on physical dominance and seniority. Forget the happy-go-lucky rules of the outside world, welcome to the jungle. You might think you're tough out there, but in here it's a different code—eye for eye, remember Hammurabi? And bowing down in submission is no way to win you respect; it's a tricky situation really, bow and submit, or hold your ground? Sticking up for yourself will either win you respect, or get your ass beaten, and sometimes pride is worth it. I think to myself, I would have never lowered myself to such a disgusting scumbag dope head like Speedy. I would have had a nice French phrase for him, *"sus ma beat!"*

We pull in to the same garage we left the courthouse from, and shuffle out of the van, one by one. Our steel ankle cuffs echo impersonally off that cold metal ramp and now we're back in the cells beneath the courtroom.

We're stripped and searched and separated into confines, three or four guys per cell. I'm put in with Jean, the 40 year-old who acts like he's 12 (call him Mark), and the kid with the shaved head and the big teeth (call him Dan). Immediately, Mark pulls tobacco and rolling papers out of his pocket. Smoking in the cells is prohibited, but criminals tend to disregard such petty rules. Mark rolls a few up as Dan keeps watch for any guards. Mark is on his third one when Dan starts waving at him to cover the shit up. Disheveled, Mark tosses his sweatshirt on top, sending tobacco gusting to the floor and one of the already rolled cracks in half. He grunts and groans, rather irked by his carelessness.

The guard comes closer, and turns to the cell opposite us, throwing someone in. When they leave, Mark hurries to clean up the mess and rectify his broken cigarette. I tell him to just wrap another paper around it and the deed is done, simple as that. He, Dan, and Jean huddle next to the toilet where a little wall gives the shitter a half-assed attempt at privacy.

They take turns keeping watch, and I sit on the bench, tired and nervous about why the hell they brought me here a day early. My mind is racing and I can't help but think they're changing the sentence bringing up new charges and all kinds of bad thoughts are sending my mind into a deteriorating frenzy, so I stand up and start to pace—my heart is racing, my mind is spinning a thousand cycles a minute wondering if I'll be sent back to those rat cages, wondering when will I be with friends and family again, wondering just how much I managed to fuck myself over this time. I'm nineteen years old in a place I don't belong; my imagination is not my friend.

They finish off the cigarette and throw the roach in the toilet. Mark limps back to the bench and sits down, angry at the world. Jean is also sitting quietly on the bench next to me, but Dan is up and smiling. He's looking for something to do, something to occupy his busy hands, he's textbook ADHD. Mark and Dan start talking quickly in French; they're all smiles about something. Mark looks at me and says something, but it's in French and I don't understand. Turns out, Dan speaks English pretty well. "Oh, man, you're American, huh? Bloods and the Crips, right bro?" *What is it with these French Canadians asking about the Bloods and the Crips? Is that really what they associate with America?* I laugh and nod, and we exchange our stories, where we've been and why we're here. Dan tells me he's a crazy motherfucker. "Like, not in here, in here you gotta just keep quiet, don't fuck around. But on the outside, man, I'm fuckin' crazy. I mean, if someone fucks with me, I'll beat their head in with a baseball bat, you know?!" he tells me, holding his hands up like he's got a bat. He's an amiable fella, and I get the impression he's talking himself up a bit to impress me. Whatever, he seems cool, and I'm starting to like him. I had been convinced I would hate the kid after I first saw him in the bullpen many nights ago. Likewise, I had been convinced I would never take to Stephen, the same could be said for so many of the people I've encountered. I guess it goes to show, don't take someone for face value; don't jump to conclusions based on your premature judgment of them. Who they are just may surprise you.

So Dan continues his story, answering the popular "whuh-chu-in-for" question. "I steal this nice car, right? Boostin' cars you know? I steal this nice BMW and I go pick up my friends. I got my girl sittin' up front, right man?

130

You know how it is, hahaha. So I got my girl up front and two of my friends in the back when a cop pulls out behind me. I was only doin' like 120 (kilometers/hour) so I was like, fuuuck! I pull over and they know I stole the car, so they arrest me right there, throw me down on the hood about to hand cuff me. But I told you, I'm crazy, right man? Big nigger's on top of me, tryin' to cuff me, and just as he grabs the cuffs I take off running! But I only got sandals on so the big nigger caught up and tackled me. But I got one last shot in. I swung my elbow back like this..." he says, going through the motions. He's talking exuberantly, and I'm managing to laugh a bit (it is a pretty funny story, and I might have laughed more if I weren't in the given situation). "So I hit the nigger right in the ear, and he starts howling like a little bitch! His partner runs up and they finally cuff me and bring me back to the car, the whole time the nigger cop is whining. 'oh, my ear, he hit me in the ear!'"

"So how long are you in for?" I ask him.

"I dunno man. My lawyer, he knows me, friend of the family. He said he could have gotten me off on most of the charges if I hadn't hit the cop. So I told him 'oh, no man! I can't go to Sorel! They'll beat me up there! They know me there and they don't like me, they wanna kill me!' It's all about acting, I'm a good actor. So I told my lawyer that he had to make sure I didn't get a prison sentence. He said he'd do the best he could, so I guess I'll find out today."

As Dan finishes his story, the guards knock on the door and call for me in that same wimpy accent from this morning. I get up, eager to leave. I'm walked from the cell back to that elevator from before, and they push me behind the Plexiglas shield and we're on our way toward purgatory. And there they are, those infamous doors, the portal back to reality. They walk me through and I'm back in the courtroom and there's Miss Gail waiting for me, hair pulled back, glasses sexy, and looking so smart it's hot (don't get on me about "womanizing" either. I have no prejudices toward either sex, but I've been away from women and the world for going on three weeks now, cut me a fucking break!). She tells me she was able to come in a day early to settle my case, and that I'll be out in no time. I'm ever grateful for her help, as it's clear she went out of her way to do this. With a big ingenuous smile, I thank her whole-heartedly. She tells me what to say and what will happen, and the case is underway. "Your honor...blah, blah, blah, blah..."

So now I'm good to go, just waiting on the border people to come pick me up and bring me back to my truck. The thing is, I gotta wait downstairs in the cells. That's not cool, not cool at all. But I'll be out by two o'clock, I guess.

So it's back through the ominous double doors, back to the elevator to take me two floors closer to hell, and back to my cell. Dan sees me and immediately starts berating me with questions. I tell him that I should be out soon, and he's anxious to see what he'll get off with.

And so I wait to be picked up and taken home—the agonizing wait where seconds creep like sun shadows and growing greenery because everything moves so slowly when we look ahead of ourselves. And when we look back we only see in fast-forward. So I remind myself to live the present, be contented and at ease, but I've had enough of this place and with my emancipation so near, it's a mind marathon from here 'til the end and this mind is running out ahead of itself—oh, tire! oh, exhaust!

And every time the guards knock, my heart skips and my eyes stare straight dead ahead, waiting in anxious anticipation for them to call my name in that whimsy French accent. But it never comes and each time is so demoralizing that I've convinced myself that I'll go insane before they come for me.

Another knock…but it's only lunch time. They throw us each two sandwiches (two pieces of white bread with one piece of cheese, and two pieces of white bread with one piece of processed ham) and a carton of milk. I put the ham and cheese together, eat the two plain slices first, saving the ham and cheese sandwich for last. The cell's silent now, save the smack-smack of barbarians feasting.

The sandwiches came wrapped in plastic, and after we finish eating, Dan asks me for the plastic wrap that came with my meal. I give it to him with an "okay…" and he says to me, "you know what this is for?" He pretends to put something in the middle and wrap it up, and with his hands he demonstrates the physics behind "phshttt…up the asshole!" So these are the people who do this sort of thing.

"Yeah, man, drugs. Put a few crack rocks in here, some weed, make money! I could sell one rock for 80 bucks in Sorel! One rock that goes for 20 on the street! Weed? 30 a gram!" *What the fuck do I say to that?!* Uhh, cool? Uhh, good for you? He changes the subject before I can think of something to say.

"Yo, you ever do crack? I smoked it once with my buddies, like…"
Picture this kid, shaved head and big ol' funny teeth, hyper out of his mind.
He demonstrates his crack experience for us. Someone get this kid an Oscar!
"AH!" he pops at us, eyes wide and tweaked out of his head, his big teeth
hanging out of his face as he screams loud as he can. So I'm laughing 'cause
this kid is hysterical, and just as the crack starts to wear off, he turns around
again and pretends to do two lines of blow. He whips around, arms out like a
cat, and pounces on the bench. He jumps onto that half wall next to the toilet
and starts to climb up top. He's yelping at the top of his lungs, and I'm bent
double with laughter. Well, his antics stir up ruckus with the guy in the cell
opposite us, and the guy starts yelling with hostility at Dan. Dan won't have
none of that, so he gets his nose right up to the window and starts hollering
back. It's angry French and they aren't playing nice. A couple of guards walk
between them to try to settle them, but end up moving the other dude
somewhere else.

I felt like I should give Dan 20 dollars or something for that show.
"You should be a standup comedian!" I tell him. He laughs and says he's
actually considered that—considered getting out of the dirty underground, the
dope dealing, the car boosting. His show helped pass the time, and pretty soon,
the guards are back, and this time they say my name. I get up and say goodbye
to Dan. He asks me to wait for him outside the courthouse (as he had found
out that he would only be given community service, and that he was being
released that same day too) but I tell him I won't be able to, they're taking me
back to the border. As I'm leaving, I think to myself that Dan is the type of kid
who would have made a good friend if I were still back at Sorel.

I'm taken down the hall and they sit me at a table to sign paperwork. Arthur, the nice guy who I met 12 days earlier at the courthouse, is there to help me out, and I'm grateful to see him and not some prick. I sign some papers, and Arthur tells me that I am technically free to go, but…he has to drive back to Sorel to get my wallet and other personal items. "Is there anything else there that you will need?" he asks.

"Yes, I had a pair of shorts, but the thing I most desperately want back is my pad of paper. It has a green cover on it, just a normal pad of paper, but I have written about 20 pages in it. It's the most important thing to me, I don't care about anything else, this has…sentimental value."

"Ok, I'll try to get that for you…no, you know what? I promise I'll get that for you!" His promise reassures me, and I thank him very much for that, but now I have to wait while he drives an hour there, an hour back, and who knows how much time at the prison itself. Still, I wasn't supposed to be getting out until tomorrow, and I'd just be waiting back in D-wing anyway. I think about the guys still in Sorel. Stephen on his "Cadillac of pills," Bear and his popsicle stick models, Shifty and his tremulous stutter. I think about D-wing, Frank and Pat, the Fag and the decrepit old man, but most of all I think of Mike and Tony—how Mike did so much for me, cans of soda, shower sandals, he was just a great guy and I didn't get the chance to thank him for everything he did. I call back to Arthur as they're leading me back to a new cell. Hobbling in my ankle and wrist cuffs, I tell Arthur to give Mike my thanks if he sees him.

For some reason, the guards take me to a new cell with no one else in it or near it. It's not so bad, in fact, I relish the silence—I can meditate and be goofy with myself, no worries of what the other guys are about to do, no cigarette smoke, nice. I sit on the bench, calm and relaxed. I close my eyes and begin to subjugate my mind; I wander off in meditation to a black void warmed by a single mellow flame. I'm at ease for the first time today, for the first time since the mountains, really. It is a great tool to be able to fall into meditation in such times. I only wish I had been more adept in it before my prison stay. As I ease out of this serenity, I feel contented to simply sit and wait and let my mind play. A half an hour passes and I look at my watch in anticipation (That watch saved me. without it, I'm sure I would have slipped slowly into senility long ago.). I'm starting to get restless again, and I try another round of meditation, but I can't coax myself to slip beneath its surface (again, I do wish I were more adept in this magnificent tool). I decide to stand up and start pacing. One-Two-Three-Stop. About face. One-Two-Three- Stop. I repeat nonsensical pattern a thousand times over and my watch is telling me it's only been twelve minutes. How much more of this waiting must I endure? I begin to read the scratched names and notes on the walls—the names of dreamers who rot away a worthless life, the thinkers who never *did!* Most are in French, but one catches my eye. "Best sex in Montreal. Call Mary xxx-xxx-xxxx." '*Best sex in Montreal, huh? Maybe I'll give her a ring when I get outta here,*' I think to myself, jokingly. The dude even scribbled that in French too, and I'm lightly amused.

So it is again, the dense, dark cloud of boredom, so thick I can feel it choking me and nothing that I do seems to help it to disperse. I feel a burst of energy now, no longer tired, so I start exercising—push-ups, sit-ups, jump-ups to the bench. And I think back to my sixth grade days when I would ski and skate and jump off of anything with the reckless abandonment of a 12 year-old daredevil. I jump up on the bench and take a few quick steps and 360 off. Next time I throw a grab in like a skater. I'm doing all kinds of petty tricks like this and laughing with myself, hushed but still aloud. It's great really; here I am making a jungle gym out of a prison cell. I tire myself out and take a seat; between the endorphins and the playtime nostalgia, I'm all smiles and suddenly this place ain't so bad anymore. It's already been an hour and a half; Arthur should be back within an hour.

I burst out in song, *"Danke Shoen, darling danke shoen…"* Any song that pops into mind, I sing it. I close my eyes and picture me back with my sweetheart, how I'm gonna sing to her as such on her birthday, how we'll dance to my awful tune, but laughing all the while because we are with each other—and then we'll be tipsy on wine and like children playing dress up in our fancy shoes and prettied clothes. And I will sing and she will smile and I'll lean in to whisper in her ear, "I like the way your eyes frown when you smile," and oh, we'll be in *lust,* won't we, my darling?

Me thinking back to home makes me all the more anxious to get out of here. The high is short and dies soon and that rueful cloud is back to taunt me. I try to lie down, to close my eyes and rest, but my mind won't have it, and these metal benches aren't exactly conducive for a nap.

Finally I see a guard; it's been two and a half hours, he's gotta be coming for me. He opens the slot on the door and I jump down and stick my wrists out for him to cuff them (just like how Norman leapt off the bench, how he knew exactly what to do). He leads me out to the main area and I take a seat at the table again.

Down the hall, another inmate is being let out, and to my left is another one. Both are cuffed at the ankles and wrists (in front) like I am. The one on my left sees the other and yells down to him in boastful instigation. I guess these two have history because the other one starts raging like he's about to kill somebody. The guy to my left just stands his ground with a goading smile, one guard holding him at each arm. Two guards walk the other inmate down the hall; he's calmed down and looks like he's cooperating. I know what's coming even before those dumb lummox guards can see it, it's obvious what this guy is about to do. Just as he is being walked by the guy on my left, he lashes out of the guards grip and sprints at the guy on my left like he's thirsty for murder. But as he starts to sprint, he trips on his ankle chain and falls face first to the cement floor, breaking his fall with his elbows and landing right at the other guy's feet. I see the guy on my left, still standing, raise his foot up as high as the chains will let him, and he sends it crashing down on the back of the fallen man's skull. I watch his face smash on the floor, I see his chin split at the seam. He rolls over in agony, hands cupping his broken jaw. And as if that weren't enough, I see the guy on my left raise his hands over his head and drop them slamming on the poor man's open face. I flinch and look away feeling sick, but not before I catch glimpse of the poor man's open eye, the gouge of flesh puking blood from his brow, sliced open by the metal of the cuffs. The guards dive in to break it up, but it's too late for the one guy. He's in critical condition, leaking blood by the quart. The guards have tazed the guy on my left into submission, but I can only concentrate on the poor man who looks as though he could lose his life right there on the spot, or at least lose his eye. His left eye is no longer visible, it is a pool of black blood, and his hands are still cupping his broken jaw, holding his head still but his lower half is wiggling in intense pain. At this point I feel truly nauseous, and I can't watch this anymore. You see this sort of thing in movies, but know it's acting and effect. And sure, you know it happens in real life, but in your candy land bubble of Suburbia, it's only fiction. Well here it is right in front of my flinching eyes. The blood pouring down the center drain the way you see in horror movies. This man is no actor, he's real and live and not for long if they don't get him some help. All guards are on deck and it's pure chaos, exacerbated by the hooting and hollering of the rambunctious inmates who watched the assault (murder?). One guard grabs me by the arm and leads me back to a cell, and I'm glad to be removed from the scene. He throws me in the same cell as before, and I'm reunited with Jean, Dan, and Mark. Dan is surprised to see me still around. "Hey man I thought you were out." I explain what happened, and they're asking all kinds of questions about what's going on outside in the hall. I give them the story with sickly disgust in my face. I can hardly think about it or I'm convinced I'll puke on the spot.

Everything quiets down, and I'm sitting again, wondering what will happen to that poor man. Arthur and one of the guards come to fetch me a half an hour later, and I walk back to that table. I glance over to the spot where it happened; it's cleaned up, not a drop of blood. But the drain is now rimmed red in dried blood that couldn't be healed, as though forever scarred by the brutality of the man. I have to sign release papers, and Arthur gives me a bag with my stuff. I look inside for the only thing that matters, my green pad…it isn't there. Arthur sees the disappointment on my face and asks, "That green pad, is it possible it's in your truck?" I bow my head in crushing melancholy and tell him no, that I bought it at the prison. I know what happened; Mike probably grabbed it off my shelf to read what else I had written since. The bag is everything from my cell, including Pat's shirt that he loaned me. The guards collected everything: they're so fucking stupid it's irritating. I ask Arthur if there is any way I can get my pad back, and he says he'll give me an address to write to in Sorel. I'm saddened, but optimistic that there will be a way to get it back. I had poured my thoughts, and the pad was a primary account of exactly how I was feeling in that moment. Oh, I desperately wanted it back!

I'm led into a holding room to be searched again before the van ride back to the border. Then it's down that metal ramp, the cold clanking of my chains, and into the van. The van is so much better without the carcinogen bath and rotting thugs. At the border, the two guards hand me over, and I'm left in a different kind of cell. I'm stripped of my shoes and shirt and thrown in a cold box, brightly lighted with white walls and a single wooden bench. The word "sanitary" comes to mind, but there's something eerie about it. In the ceiling, a camera watches everything I do. My feet are starting to ache from the chill of the lonely cell. I can't sleep or even rest and this is misery. Now, I have paid my dues, done my time, and I'm supposed to have been free. Why all of this? An hour I wait before I catch one guard's attention with the excuse that I have to use the latrine. He lets me out and I cooperate (as I have done throughout this entire ordeal). As he's letting me back into the cell, I ask him how much longer. He says it won't be long. I hate ambiguous answers.

Another torturous hour of restlessness passes. I stand up off the bench and I'm doing the One-Two-Three-Stop. About face. One-Two-Three-Stop thing again. I stop and stare at a shadow on the wall and strike up a conversation with my new lonely friend. The shadow's name is Louis, but he tells me I can call him Louie. He grew up in Alberta, and I ask him about the Canadian Rockies. He used to hunt the vast fields for elk and moose and he tells me a funny story of how he and his father (now deceased) were once chased up trees by a bull moose. I'm literally standing with my nose four inches from the wall, carrying on a conversation with a shadow like he's my best friend when the guard opens the door. Tell me I've teetered on the brink of dementia, and I'll say you have no idea.

I'm escorted into an office, still half naked and chilled, to sign papers and find out what to do from here. The first thing they tell me is that I don't have enough money to get my truck back (as they had run up 700 DOLLARS OF FALLACIOUS CHARGES!) I'm burning with hatred and outrage at this point. But I grit my teeth and keep a calm head about my shoulders. The next thing this guard tells me is that I am banned from Canada forever. Yes, I am banned from Canada, forever. But the thing that really set me off was that he made my sign a paper that said, "This person (meaning me) is, *in my opinion, unfit for Canada." In your opinion? IN YOUR MOTHERFUCKING WORTHLESS OPINION I AM NOT WORTHY OF CANADA? You French pig, you rat bastard fucking slug of a human life. How dare you soil my good name with your filthy opinion when you've never even seen me before in your life. You know what? Fuck you! Fuck you and your god damn country. My sole purpose of existence is to spread truth, knowledge and happiness. I have never done anything unethical since I was old enough to know the difference, but I'm the one unfit for* your *country? FUCK YOU and* "tar ba nock!"

141

He slides the paper over for me to sign, and at this point I'm smoking from the ears. I grind teeth together and pick up the pen, slow and easy. The paper is one of those long, winded documents in size eight font with a line for you to sign at the bottom. I stare the motherfucker dead in his eyes as I sign my name big and proud across the whole fucking paper. He isn't amused.

I'm told that I will be taken back to the U.S. border, and another guard takes his cuffs out. I look from the cuffs to him and back to the cuffs in disbelief. I have done my time and cooperated politely throughout. I'm a free man now, these cuffs are just unnecessary. What am I going to do? Run off when I'm literally two minutes from my home? They ask me if I would like anything out of my truck; I ask for my rucksack and my book. The rucksack should have all my survival gear, and I have a long road to walk or hitchhike or freight train hop ahead of me so I'll certainly need it. Well, wouldn't you know it, the bastard pig who *in his opinion* deemed me unfit for his puke of a country is the one to cuff me and lead me out. He's holding me by the arm and using more force than necessary as he leads me through a door and into a lobby where innocent civilians, families and all, wait to cross into Canada. And here I am, insolent and fighting back for the first time because this is grossly unjust. I'm throwing my elbow into this asshole's gut and walking fast then slow, and I see these families hold their precious children close and pray that their kids don't turn out like "that bad man (me)." I think back to the days of my youth when I would see a "bad man" being arrested and my mother would hold me close as though to preserve my innocence with the magic of a mother's touch, and she would tell me, "look, those are bad men, they're being taken to jail." And now, here I am, the "bad man" and the idea makes me want to cry. I choke back the tears as I throw another elbow into the abhorrent pig to hear him squeal and they throw me in the back of the car.

As we drive up to the U.S. border, I'm asked if I was treated ok in Canada. Hmm...

Finally I'm back home, safe under the warm blanket of good old Uncle Sam, and oh, it feels so good! The French fucks hand me my rucksack, and it's not full like it should be. When I grab it, I notice it's heavy as hell too. I open it up and feel that burning hatred course my spine, and I break out in cold sweat. Those useless pigs gave me my rucksack filled with the small library of classic literature I had in my truck. There is no sleeping bag, no tent, no rain poncho. There is no long underwear, no food, no Camelback. But I do have forty pounds worth of Hemmingway, Dostoevsky, London, Irving, Kerouac, Tolstoy, Nietzsche, Rousseau and others. I'm so exhausted, so infuriated, so lost that I feel myself drowning in the abyss of human extremes. This is the breaking point, and I could burst out in tears right now and have myself a sorrowful cry for forty-five minutes. I could sob and sob, feeling sorry for myself and what I've had to go through and what lies ahead of me. But that would just accomplish nothing, and so I bite down hard and feel the burn of crying in my jaw. I swallow hard and fight back tears knowing that if I let myself break, the 400 mile trek back to Rochester will be that much harder.

So I pull myself together and make chummy with the U.S. border people. The difference in candor between these good men and women and the scum that slithers on the other side is immense. These officers are amiable and willing to help. We trade stories and they understand that I'm not such a bad guy after all. I tell them I'll be at the prestigious West Point this coming summer, how that is my next adventure, and this detail helps to solidify, in their eyes, the notion that I'm a good kid with a kind heart. They even buy me a sandwich out of the vending machine, and I am so grateful to be back into the hospitable arms of decent people. The sandwich was some much needed sustenance for the road journey ahead of me. At midnight, a greyhound bus headed about fifteen miles south into Plattsburgh pulls up. The U.S. border officers talk to the driver, who sympathizes with my story and offers me a free ticket into the small town. I climb aboard, very grateful that such kind people exist. When the bus pulled into Plattsburgh, I was the last to get off; relishing the soft seat I had managed to doze off in. Once everyone else had evacuated, I walked up and gave the driver my sincerest thank you. He nodded "no problem" and told me he had been inspired by my story, my "pursuit of happiness." This brilliant bus driver had just used those coveted words from the Declaration of Independence, and I was speechless. I had never thought of my adventures in such a profound light, but it was apparent that some people did. *My pursuit of happiness—my declaration of independence.* Suddenly there it was, the grandiose meaning behind what I was doing put so simply, so profoundly. I think back to my friends Leo and Charity, the Christian miracle, the saints and saviors whom I met during my trans-America journey a few months ago. I think about how I left them, touched spiritually by their devout praise for Jesus, and how they had cared so genuinely for all of his children. I think about how humble and happy they were, the epitome of love and oh, it was so beautiful to see such simple and sincere love! And how they called me Devine for what I was doing, for my fearless inspiration to seek the beauty and truth hidden beneath the sour crust of this world. They told me that the bible says to always be kind to strangers, for you never know if a stranger is a lost angel come to seek your help. They thought I was the angel, but I saw them as something more.

But now I see the inspiring theme. People are seeing my journeys as inspirational, the same way I had pictured they would be for me. And if my stories will inspire, then I want to spread them far and wide. This is when I decide to write the books.

16

Plattsburgh is cold tonight, but the sky is clear and the wind is only at a whisper. I walk into the bus station and pull my ripped and torn pants up over my wrestling shorts, the same pants that spent a week with me climbing mountains and living off the land of the Adirondacks. They're caked in dirt, but comfortable and loose and better than no pants. I wander the streets of this desolate town with no place to go and nothing to do. Here I am with this big peculiar back pack on, walking into a sad bar in a back alley, but the sign hung awkwardly and the old wood and chipped paint looked too perfect in the moonlight for me not to patron this place. Inside is a long bar with a lone tender, two tables for two and one for four, and a dart board (all the dart tips broken). It's one o'clock by now, and the man behind the bar, apparently the owner, is washing mugs and closing up. I sit at the bar with the defeated look of man returned from battle, me and my big ruck sack filled with books and nothing useful for survival. I pull out my copy of *The World According to Garp* by John Irving, and begin to lose myself in a world that isn't this one (any world but this one). The owner is a graying man, maybe sixty, with a white beard and a wise look. He pours me a beer and asks me what my story is. By now I'm so sick of the story that I can't fathom running through it one more time, but I like the look of this man, and he gave me a free beer.

     I start from the beginning. I tell him about living off the Adirondack land, about the high peaks and their salvation. I tell him about the Canada debacle, and how I'm stuck now with no money, no ride, and no will power left in me. The whole time he looks at me with those wise, pensive blue eyes, as though empathizing with what I had just been through. He pours himself a tall glass, and hands me another and we get drunk and talk like old wise men. I'm ranting on about society's labels and boring people all trying to be the same thing, afraid of themselves or something. Before I know it, I'm pouring my heart out about the girl back home whom I just can't forget about—the girl I love and she don't love me back and oh, what a tumultuous ride it has been! We talk broken mirrors and shattered hearts and how there's so much more to this world than heartache and misery. How the two are necessary and inevitable, and how we're better off having experienced them, but he tells me life goes on. He tells me to go about my ways, and the rest (including the girl) will fall into play. "When you're up, it's never as good as it feels, and when you're down you think you'll never get back up. And the rest of the time, we're just coasting." Well, we're on our fourth tall one and I'm near tears again. I thank him and tell him I have no money, but he just looks at me understandingly and says, "I know."

I leave the bar with a final goodbye and a handshake, thinking that's the kind of man I want to be, with insightful and understanding wisdom. I'm back on the street under the cold moonlight and the buzz from the alcohol gives the town a Romantic shimmer. I wander down the sidewalk of the sullen streets of Plattsburgh and the rows of 1970 houses, all different and all the same, that big ruck sack clapping its straps to the rhythm of my shuffle. All around me stagger groups of friends living their own version of the alcoholic diaries, laughing deep into the limitless night while I scowl trapped inside a cynical void. I watch a couple walk on heavy drunken feet, a tall and lank black man who walks with a crippled limp and his squat white girlfriend. They embody a trashy stereotype and I stare livid under a sharp brow, criticizing them for what I think they are—here I am, preaching insight and empathy, yet watching these people in blinded prejudice thinking, "Oh what scum. And people like them *procreate*...disgusting. Throw another family on the welfare system and I'll pay for this slug to sit on his ass and watch TV." But they're happy and that's the only thing we can do in this life, make it through the chutes and ladders with as much happiness as we can.

I eventually find my way back to the bus stop, and it's already four a.m.—the deathly sad hour of four a.m. Outside the bus station, I take a seat on a bench, dizzy and mystified from the alcohol. Above me lies a blanket of stars and a vast universe where something so subtle as my misery and heartache just don't matter and I wonder why it means so much to me, how something so insignificant can truly hurt so bad. It isn't fair, nothing has been fair or just or *right!* I've worked so hard all my life to be shit on by fate a thousand times over, and now, everything I thought I was working so hard for is just insignificant. Wise stars stare down at lonely me and they tell me, everything I've ever done and everything I ever will do, every emotion and all my pain and even my happiness, it means nothing. Oh welkin vanity and cloud shrouded cynicism, behind us mimics the pseudo-revels of a dear Eastern Eden. Here where the grey tears of a smoky soul weep nourishing to kindle new growth, and we see the world turn from vacant eyes, the circle of life that has warped elliptical and off track. We see the sullen lands stretched vast across a shimmering America that we can only look back on with jaded eyes because all that exists now are the plagued fields of our own jealous plight— the tragic woes of anger and pugnacity, so primitive and all expected but it's just no way to go through life! Maybe let us behave as can only be expected, maybe we *aren't* better than the fucking and the fighting so let us act on rage and primitive passion? Maybe we were never meant to overcome such things. Instead, the ideals and ethical codes are just an arrogant rendition of one man and his narcissism. But in such a seemingly purposeless life where all we can do it pass through it with as much happiness as we can, there exists only one responsibility, our only definite contribution—an obligation, and our one true purpose is to spread as much joy and laughter as we can to the people who walk through the same game at our side.

And now I just can't choke back the tears and so I let them pour, I cry and cry for everything. I cry for the hard work that never paid off, for the injustices of life and the setbacks of this year alone, and I cry for how I didn't deserve them. I cry for the girl I loved and for the girl I love now, and how neither of them loved me back and *why wasn't I good enough?* I cry even harder because I feel so stupid sitting here crying, and I pull and tear at the straps on my ruck sack, holding back my masochism because all I want to do it hurt myself right now for all I'm not worth, for how pathetic I really am. Oh, give me rain to hide my tears and lightning to strike my sorrows!

But there is no rain this cold spring night. Only me and my thundering sobs. I pull myself together and walk into the nearly deserted bus station to find a corner to sleep in.

17

Only a couple hours later I awaken to a bright and motivating sun
shining down on me through the small window as though checking up on me,
its slumbering child. But I hardly feel so fresh, my mouth parched and stale
and my head aching—hangover from the night before. I search through my
ruck sack again and find what I was looking for; at least those French pigs
gave me my toiletries bag. I pull out my toothbrush and paste and try to wash
the skunked taste off of my tongue. It's only 7:30 a.m., but I decide I had
better get moving, so I pack back up and haul off toward I-87.

The sun is warm, but the breeze stings and I'm wishing my jeans
weren't so torn up. The interstate isn't very busy, so I start to walk south,
thumb out at every passing vehicle. I walk all damn day and around two
o'clock I stop to rest. I haven't eaten or slept much in the past couple of days,
and now it's catching up on me. I feel light headed from low blood sugar and

I'm starting to think last night's beer was an awful idea. My vision starts to get hazy, I'm seeing dots, so I take my ruck sack off and lean against the guard rail, but now I'm feeling dizzy and weak, so I hop the rail and lie down on my back to let it pass. I pull my ruck sack over slowly by the strap and reach my hand into my toiletries bag, desperate for some sort of nourishment, anything to raise my blood sugar and end this nausea—I wish I had juice. I break out in a cold sweat, I feel like I am burning up, but I'm shivering violently, or maybe just shaking. The cool wind seems to have stopped blowing just when I need the fresh air most.

With my hand rummaging blindly through the toiletries bag, I find a godsend, a plastic bag filled with some sort of nuts, the half finished trail mix left over from my time in the mountains! Slowly I pull the bag out so as not to spill anything and lay it on my chest. I eye the raisins and m&m's first, being the fastest source of sugar. Once I've picked through all of those, I begin to eat the cashews and peanuts one at a time. A slow and ill half an hour later, I'm starting to feel a bit better. I slowly sit up, now very thirsty. I'm quickly dehydrating, and though it isn't hot out, I need to find water before my dehydration advances much further. The lands are rich with greenery and foliage all around me, and I know a scene like this has got to have a running stream or waterfall of some sort. I venture away from the interstate into the wooded North Country, ears perked up for the sound of running water.

A half a mile off the throughway, the woods abruptly stop, yielding farm land and a horse ranch. To my left I see the farm house, but I'm not keen on knocking on the door looking like a lost Brahman. As I near the house, I see a garden hose coiled up around a sprinkler, and I begin to walk more

152

quickly. I drop my bag at the edge of the wood line and creep closer to the house, weary of guard dogs and trigger-happy farmers. I reach the side of the house and kneel in the mud around the hose spigot, and slowly turn it on to just a trickle. The cold water pours so sweetly over my dried and cracking lips and I savor every drop. One reaches a point of dehydration where he will do anything for just a drink. Nothing but *water* matters at that point, because anything else is too thick to swallow anyway. I had experienced this dreadful threshold while sucking weight for wrestling back in high school, and it was a point I thought I would never reach again.

Well, here I am, sucking at the water like a glutton, feeling every drop gush into my dehydrated mouth and throat. I sip slowly at first, but soon give in to the urge to gulp and gulp away. I turn the hose on more powerfully and let the stream of water force fill my mouth and I would gulp that holy nectar down, and then let it fill me again. I take short breaks in between drinking to catch my breath and let the water settle, then I fill my mouth again, knowing the importance of hydration as both a physical and mental boost. Once saturated, I turn the nozzle off and creep away back to my rucksack, then steal into the woods feeling the surge of hope that always comes with rehydration and a midday snack—now if only I could nap. I walk back through the woods, pulling that awkward ruck sack full of books through the thick, and soon I am back at the interstate walking south, thumb held out high and proud.

The sun begins to set and still I've had no luck hitching. I'm discouraged, my feet are blistered and sore, my shoulders are tight and my head is throbbing. I feel my hips and knees start popping and I just want to be *home!* As the daylight slips away, it dawns on me that if I don't get a ride, I'm

153

stuck in the cold scary night, alone and with nothing. I can honestly say that I am afraid –terrified– *what will I do? How will I make it* alive*?!* It's nearly night time now, and at this point I'm stumbling wearily and weak, any moment I could pass out and not even know it. And just when I have knocked on the door of my breaking point, here comes a big semi-trailer lumbering down the highway. I stick my thumb out and stop in my tracks, turning to face the white of the headlights. The truck roars by and now I start to panic. Several odd things have happened to me on these trips, odd things that hint at fate. I had given up on such things; I stopped believing in God some time ago. But fate was always different. I had been hesitant to actually give up on the idea of *fate*. And as fate or maybe just coincidence could have planned, I saw the big semi trailer's brake lights flash on, bright in the darkening night, I heard his brake pads whine and screech as the truck slowed, and I saw the orange blinker flashing canorously. The truck was pulling over! This big black beast in the dreary night would be my salvation!

I hustle with all my energy up to the truck and reach for the door handle. I pull the door open and I meet eye to eye with a grungy looking fella. Before I have anytime to say something, he looks at me and says, "Just so you know, boy, you try anything funny you're a dead man!" brandishing a small revolver. The guy scares the shit out of me, but what else can I do but say, "yes, sir." I throw my ruck sack in on the passenger side floor and climb into the seat. I ask him where he's heading and he tells me New York City. I ask if he's going through Albany, he is, so I ask him to drop me off there.

"You got it, kid. So what are you doing out on the open road with that army bag you got there?" he asks, nodding a black bearded chin at my ruck sack. I told him I had been camping in the mountains but I had run out of food and got lost trying to find my truck. I said I had spent all of yesterday walking east looking for the interstate, and all of today trying to hitch a ride.

"Well, what you goin' back to Albany for? Don't you have to get your truck back?"

I had slipped up. I hadn't thought it all through. I knew I would just dig my grave deeper if I tried to talk my way out of this one. I changed the subject saying, "I'm real tired, you mind if I nap 'til we get to Albany?" I knew this made him suspicious, but he didn't ask any more questions.

We drive through the night and I sleep the whole way to Albany. When we get to the intersection of I-87 and I-90, the driver wakes me up. "All right kid, I'll pull over here. You sure you'll be alright?" he asks, seeming genuine in his concern.

I thank him for the ride and he wishes me luck on the rest of my trip, "whatever it is you're doin'!" I hop down and close the door, shoulder my ruck sack, and walk off half-asleep and half-awake toward the toll booths. It's only one in the morning, and now I'm stuck in the same terrifying predicament as before, but at least this time there are buildings and people around to help. I'm looking for a diner or something that is open for 24 hours, but I don't see anything around. I do see some office buildings maybe a mile away. So I set off, tired and beaten and not done yet. The first two buildings I try are locked. The third sits bleak in its yellow light, an eerie thing and brilliant set for a nightmare. The building's door in unlocked and I walk into a small lobby. The doors off the lobby are all locked, but there are stairs in the lobby, so I climb up the stairs. At the top, there is a small area about 1x2 meters, and another door, also locked. At this point I'm just grateful for the shelter and warm(er) area to stay. I lay my rucksack in the corner and use it as a pillow. I have reached a point so low that all I want is a roof to sleep under. Of course I'm nervous about the trespassing, the breaking into the office, but at this point I'm so desperate that my truancy is the least of my worries.

18

In the morning I wake up in a strange place and remember that I'm in an office building. It's only seven a.m., thankfully, or I could be waking up to another arrest and hand cuffs. I hear the lobby door open and I freeze, my heart racing, eyes wide and ears perked up. For a minute or so, I only hear footsteps walking around the lobby, no first floor doors open, but no footsteps up the stairs either. I consider calling out in case they do come up the stairs so I don't scare them half to death, but at the moment I'm plain petrified. The seconds tick tense, and finally I hear a first floor door open. I peak over the balcony and see a man in a suit walking into one of the doors. *That's it*, I decide. *I gotta get out of here!* I grab the ruck sack, shoulder it, and quietly glide down the stairs and through the door. The morning is brisk but sunny, and the sun is all the motivation I need for now. I make my way back to the thruway and past the toll booths, hoping for better luck on the road today than I had had in the past.

I walked until noon and covered maybe ten miles before I got my first break of the day. A white semi trailer, alone on the open road, saw my thumb and pulled off a hundred meters down the road for me. A minute later I was looking up into the eyes of a stout, friendly looking woman in the passenger seat. "Hi there, need a lift?" she asked, big smile perking rosy cheeks, red hair frazzled in the wind.

"I sure do, where are you headed?" I ask.

"We're headed to Utica for a quick stop, then we'll be passin' through buffalo and on our way to Toronto."

"Well I'm going to Rochester, and if it's no trouble, I'd love a ride!"

"Alright, well hop on in; we have some room in the back here. Oh, and just so you know, we have mace…"

She climbed out of her seat and hopped down to let me in. I hauled my ruck sack up the steps and I see her husband (so I assumed) at the wheel. Behind their seats was a good amount of space, enough for my ruck sack and me to sit comfortably. I climbed back and the wife jumped back in and we were off West—like pioneers of the wild frontier. I just wanted sleep, but the couple was eager to hear my story. I told them something about how I had wanted to travel across the country but didn't have much money. I told them I had been hopping freight trains and hitchhiking for the past three days and had made it all the way from Guilford, CT. I spoke in monotone, half on purpose to bore them out of talking to me and half because that was all the voice I could muster.

I'm happy to be off the hungry road and riding along some place I can sit, but now all I want is some rest and silence. The couple eventually runs out of questions and truck driving stories and I begin to nod off. But only a short while later, the wife wakes me saying, "We gotta make a quick stop in Utica if that's alright with you. Shouldn't take more than an hour if you wanna wait, up to you."

"I open my eyes, startled at where I am having mixed dream and reality in that delicate stage between REM and real. "Oh, sure I'll stay, I'm patient. Hey, do you guys need any help with anything?"

"Oh, no but thanks for the offer! We just have to do an inspection." They pull off the ramp and drive that monstrous trailer through the little streets of downtown Utica with impressive agility and generous use of the horn. They stop the truck and hop out and I jump out too to stretch my legs. The husband has to run inside, but the wife stays back with me to hold the fort. I'm pacing around in a pensive silence, inspecting the wear and tear on my knees and hips for the beatings they've taken on the grueling hikes. My left knee pinches tender at the meniscus anytime I completely straighten it, but I figure it's just a minor over use issue. I walk around the lumbering trailer, observing all the gears and gadgets that get that thing hauling. I circle around the back and head up toward the cab, my mind empty, and just kind of *looking*. At the door, I catch a glimpse of my face in those bulky side mirrors and do a double take. I walk up close and stare at my own face, startled and remembering what I used to look like. I haven't seen my face in nearly three weeks, and it is as if I have forgotten what I look like. I stare into the tired eyes of a weathered man—wise eyes that have seen so much. I see his unkempt hair wild and rebellious. His jaw is strong and his cheeks don't smile, but he looks contented in his tired eyes. A young beard grows off his chin and the sides of his cheeks, and elsewhere he is bare because he is still just a kid—he'd be a handsome kid if he cleaned himself up, but dirt shadows across his forehead and his cheeks are pulled in sullenly making his eyes dark and hollow and vacant. I have seen this face before, it is the starved face of the dog days of cutting weight, sucked out and still two pounds over, the same tired eyes, the same sunken cheeks. The only thing new is the wanderer's beard that stubbles my chin.

Only a half an hour later, the husband returns and we saddle up ready to go. I climb in back again and we get rolling toward the thruway. The entire winding way through the Utica streets, the husband and wife have no more questions, nothing more to say. But by the time we pass the toll booths, they are full of little anecdotes and asking me about my experiences. But I just want to *sleep*. I answer their questions as shortly and unenthusiastically as I can, and by the time we are nearing Syracuse, their badgering has stopped and I can crash out, head propped against the back of the seat, legs sprawled atop my ruck sack. The next time the wife speaks to me she's telling me we have made it to Rochester. Rochester! I never thought I would be so excited for Rochester in my life, but here I was, I had made it to *Rochester!*

They let me off at the exit ramp junction and I thank them with a bright and gracious smile and they go on their way, giving me three cheerful honks with the foghorn. I am probably less than 15 miles from home, but my last meal was those nuts from the old trail mix, and my last drink was at the hose. I haven't slept much either, and the combination of all the factors are pulling and dragging at my body. A 15 mile walk with my ruck sack, in this condition, could take three more days. And so I begin. I take I-490 toward the city, thumb stuck out and hoping for the best.

Right out of the toll booths, not a half a mile up, a car pulls off a hundred feet ahead of me. It is a dark green Saturn with two heads in the front seat. I hustle up quickly and peer into the window, not saying anything yet. Inside, a young woman is driving and a man sits in the passenger seat, they're maybe 24.

"We're headed into the city if you need a ride." The city would take me even further out of the way, but I might be able to catch the RTS bus and take that back home, and I am not looking forward to a 15 mile march either. I jump in, eager for another story, and we're on our way. The girl tells me how she and her boyfriend, Victor, have experience in hitchhiking, so they understand what I am going through. She wears a loose shawl with a beautiful and ornate paisley pattern, and her hair hangs over her dark eyes every time she turns back to look at me. She isn't gorgeous, but there is something attractive in her face—the dark eye that winks at me through her jungle hair, the Persian shawl that wraps around her neck, maybe it's the curious dimples in her full cheeks (she's always smiling). She's all about "green" and "oh, everything is just so *green,* like…" Victor is more reserved. He tells me he comes from Bulgaria, and he speaks in a thick Eastern European accent through large lips and a crooked nose. His hair is obviously a "did it myself catastrophe," a massacre really—shaved at the sides or here and there, but long on top and across the front, and I'm under the impression that it hasn't been washed in several days. He tells me stories of Istanbul and how Turkey had been the easiest country to hitchhike through. We exchange ideas and

161

thoughts, and for being Bulgarian, Victor speaks excellent and complicated English. He talks about rambling blues and the struggles of the road; how one learns so much about himself on the relentless and unforgiving road. When they reach their destination, we say our goodbyes and part ways. As I cross the road, Victor turns around and shouts back to me, "Thanks for carrdying thee spirit!" in his thick accent.

I'm only two blocks from the Mid-town bus stop, and I walk the whole way there with a smile ear to ear. The sky is overcast, but I am free and nearly *home* and there is no suppressing this smile. I'm watching all around me, I stare into the sky at the famous buildings of downtown Rochester, the buildings I had grown up with. I watch free people walk the sidewalk, families with babies in strollers, a man and woman walking hand in hand – her head on his shoulder as they pass me. It is all so beautiful and sweet and oh, I'm just glad to be *home!*

At Mid-town, I figure out the best bus route. The green line will take me within four miles of my father's house, and I decide to take that option – and then I remember that I have no money. I'm so beaten by this point that falling a dollar short of a warm bed and full stomach and a hug in the arms of my loving mother is devastating. I consider asking around for a quarter here and there, but that would make me a beggar and a mooch and no matter how down I am, I will always pull myself back up—self-sufficiency—I got myself into this debacle; I'll earn my way out of it with pride and dignity. I consider doing some sort of work or a favor for somebody for a dollar, but the bus is already insight, the last line running for the day. I walk over to the bus and ask the driver how much a ticket is. Maybe it was my exhausted eyes, maybe it was my sullen cheeks and sunken face, or maybe it was the way I hobbled with that ruck sack on my back (so out of place), but the bus driver took a long look at me and told me, "It's ok, Son, don't worry about it."

"Thank you so much, sir." I pull my aching body up the stairs and lay my ruck sack on the bus floor under my feet, collapsing into a seat and leaning my head against the window, watching the world exist, with a shy smile.

The bus rolls to the rhythm of its humming diesel engine and the "pshhhh" of the brakes. I sit leaning my head against the window as we drive by the parks I used to play Little League in or the fields that hosted our homecoming football games and now I'm just so relieved to be here. My mind is clear and at ease as the bus bounces stop to stop. And now the bus is passing right behind my grandmother's apartment complex and I think I might jump off right here. But if my grandma isn't home, then I'm stuck for who knows how long. And so it comes down to either taking the risk and hoping Mema is home, or riding the bus into Bushnell's Basin where I'd have a 4+ mile march back to my father's house, to be followed by a good old fashioned ass kicking. As the bus comes to its stop, I decide to jump out and take the first option. I walk through the land of cookie-cutter homes, each one exactly like the last, trying to find the right group of numbers. And there it is, the parking lot in front of her place and where is her car? Please let her car be in the lot! It is!

I shuffle up the sidewalk and knock with such exuberance on her door in the familiar da—da—da-da–da…da—da. tune and from inside I hear her asking, "who is it?" and I don't know whether to break down and cry or jump for joy at the sound of her voice and my freedom and now I'm *home* and *safe* in the hug of my dear old Mema, the grandmother who would never say no and loves me and all her children dearly beyond the vastness of the horizon where wise men sit in rocking chairs to puff at their corn pipes thinking "oh what a world we live in." I see Mema hunched in her little rocker with that unwavering smile and a tear at the crook of her eye as she peers down at her children with unquestioning love. She opens the door to see her lost grandson there hungry for her salvation and grabs me at the neck with surprising strong arms—arms that spent her youth years hauling hay and baling straw, arms that cranked at the steering wheel of a school bus, for a lifetime she did it and never complained and look at me, can't finish a year at school, college dropout bum of a grandson but to her it don't matter—just there she was to work her eighty hours or there she was with soup and bread when I was sick with migraines and Dunkaroo's watching black and white TV in her first floor den on the pullout sofa, my little feet in tiny socks and barely stretching halfway past the covers but there she was and there she always would be and here she is now, the never dying love is her one true bane. Now, how can you beat people like her? And in this moment I feel the elated peak of all metaphysical reasoning, I'm riding the cresting wave—the Nirvana of enlightenment and its own revolution—the wonderment of true humility in our mortality because I had watched blackened shadows cower in retreat from the cloak of Death itself as he ticked his finite clock to the rhythm of my own dying heart and sucked me deeper into the black emptiness of a spiritual realm. And carrying my hurting soul was the whiteness of eternal light, the Doven Angels we all carry deep within our mind body and soul, their radiant whispers that twist and turn through the warping vortexes of a tumultuous mind because thought and existence is a spider web of fate—forking choices—and were we to choose wrong we would hear only the hollow click of death's time clock snapped shut – time's up – game over – the end, the collapse of a wasted life.

www.ingramcontent.com/pod-product-compliance
Lightning Source LLC
Chambersburg PA
CBHW060420260626

47161CB00005B/1705